The
Unforgiven Hand

Perry Schwartz

The Unforgiven Hand
Copyright © 2024 by Perry Schwartz

Library of Congress Control Number: 2024906419
ISBN-13: Paperback: 978-1-64749-982-2
ePub: 978-1-64749-983-9

All rights reserved. No part of this publication may be reproduced, distributed, or transmitted in any form or by any means, including photocopying, recording, or other electronic or mechanical methods, without the prior written permission of the publisher or author, except in the case of brief quotations embodied in critical reviews and certain other noncommercial uses permitted by copyright law.

Although every precaution has been taken to verify the accuracy of the information contained herein, the author and publisher assume no responsibility for any errors or omissions. No liability is assumed for damages that may result from the use of information contained within.

Printed in the United States of America

GoToPublish LLC
1-888-337-1724
www.gotopublish.com
info@gotopublish.com

CONTENTS

Dedication		v
Chapter 1	Accounts for Trevor Going on a Trip to Key West and What He Thought of It	1
Chapter 2	An Unusual Interview, Which Is Also the Sequel to the Previous Chapter	11
Chapter 3	Describes a Shocking Secret about Trevor's Past, as Narrated by Spyder to Pastor Swanson and His Wife	21
Chapter 4	Gives in Greater Detail Another Conspiracy Created by Three Sinister Foes That the Reader Is Already Acquainted with and the Proclamation Made to Mr. Albert Swindle by Spyder	31
Chapter 5	Contains Fresh Discoveries of Trevor's Family Tree and Something Incredible Is Revealed	41
Chapter 6	Two Old Enemies of Trevor Run Away to Miami and Get a Tempting Offer from a Familiar Character	51
Chapter 7	Describes How Ezra Cooper and Zoey Were Employed by Mr. Albert Swindle	61
Chapter 8	Tells How Red Stranger Got Himself into Trouble	71
Chapter 9	Unravels the Storyline of How Ezra Was Chosen to Do a Job for Mr. Albert Swindle	81
Chapter 10	A Secret Midnight Gathering	91

Chapter 11	Unfolds the Plot of How Trevor Was Brought Back into the Clutches of Mr. Albert Swindle... 101
Chapter 12	The Great Rescue 111
Chapter 13	Brock Ferguson Finds Out Something Shocking and Takes Action 121
Chapter 14	A Promise Kept 131
Chapter 15	Illustrates Trevor Discovering the Truth about His Parents and the Circumstances behind What Really Happened on the Night of His Birth 143
Chapter 16	The Final Showdown 153
Chapter 17	Trevor Returns to His Place of Birth and Gets Retribution for How He Was Treated 167
Chapter 18	Albert Swindle's Last Day Alive 177
Chapter 19	Coming Full Circle 187
Chapter 20	At Last 197

DEDICATION

This book is dedicated in loving Memory of my good friend Samatha Eliades as she will always our hearts

CHAPTER 1

Accounts for Trevor Going on a Trip to Key West and What He Thought of It

As the month wore on, Trevor had acquired some new skills, such as cooking eggs. He learned this in only a few weeks after being shown how to do it a few times. It became much easier until he was able to make his own breakfast with no help at all. The next thing that Trevor wanted to learn how to do was play chess. He had seen the set that had been in the house since it was first built but had never been used before. The set had lots of dust all over it from just sitting there and not getting used. Now that June was almost halfway over and there was only one week left in the month, it meant that summer wasn't over just yet. There was still time to utilize all that there was to do during this fun and carefree season of the year.

On another rainy day, Trevor was in the middle of a game of chess with Margaret. She had taught him how to play, having learned from her father. "It looks like I might win. Then we will be tied at two wins each," Trevor began. "Not so fast. I have something that could ensure I beat you. Let's see if it will work," Margaret said, and she made her move. But Trevor countered with the final and winning move, breaking the tie. "Can we play again?" asked Trevor. "I don't see why not. Rhonda is busy paying the bills in the kitchen, and our uncle is on a long-distance call in his room. So let's have a rematch. I bet this time, I will beat you," Margaret answered.

Before they could start another game, the door to Norman's room opened, and he went downstairs to see what everyone was up to. The first place that he went to was where Trevor and Margaret were. "It looks like you're getting very good at playing chess. Maybe when I have time, we can play against each other. But fair warning, I'm quite the tough opponent," Norman said. "Trevor, I need to talk to you," Norman told him. "Did I do something wrong, sir?" inquired Trevor. "If you will follow me to my office, I will explain everything. Then we must be alone for you to better understand," Norman replied.

Trevor went with Norman into his office. When they got there, Trevor sat down in one of the chairs while Norman sat at his desk. "If I did something wrong, then I'm very sorry. Please don't send me back to those bad people who I was with before. I won't go and will do anything if you will let me stay. I'll be a good little boy, you won't have to worry about me," Trevor began. "No, it's quite the contrary. I need you to go up to the attic to find something for me. I have a flashlight for you to take with you so that you can see," Norman said. "What is it that I'm looking for, sir?" asked Trevor. "An old family photo album that I think is somewhere in an old trunk. It shouldn't be too hard to find, although there's a lot of stuff up there," Norman replied.

He then noticed a look of apprehension on Trevor's face. "Sir, I would like to do it. However, I'm not sure that I can," Trevor added. "Why is that?" asked Norman. "Because I'm afraid of the dark, and if I were to go up there alone, it would only frighten me more. Unless someone can come with me," Trevor answered. "That's completely understandable. Since I finished my phone call and don't have anything else to do for a few hours, I will go with you," Norman told him. "Where is the attic?" inquired Trevor. "It's upstairs, just a little bit from your room. Let's head up there now, and remember, there's nothing in the dark that can hurt you," Norman replied.

Once there, they looked around. Trevor wasn't so afraid because Norman was with him, which made him feel safer. "What's that over there?" asked Trevor, shining the flashlight at something afar. They went over to it. "That's just an old portrait of my younger sister, Grace. She died a very long time ago. Come to think of it, I hadn't heard from her in years. The last I heard about her, she fell in love and got married to some man. They didn't even have the decency to invite me to their wedding," Norman replied.

"Why is that, sir?" inquired Trevor. "They didn't say. I guess we just grew apart, like a lot of siblings do. All I ever wanted was to say 'I love you' to her one more time but never got the chance. It still haunts me to this day. I loved her just as much as she did me, even though as we became adults, it showed less, especially for her," Norman answered. "That's a very sad story; I feel sorry for you, sir. I'm sure if you could have done it, she would have been delighted to hear you say that," Trevor began.

"She was very pretty. That much I can say with all honesty and can see why all of the males were crazy about her," Norman said. "What do you think?"

"I think you're right, sir. She was a very pretty woman. Any man would have been lucky to have had her as a wife," Trevor replied.

"You know, when we were younger, Grace and I shared a room. Sometimes we'd stay up well into the night, talking about our problems, only to be yelled at by our parents in the next room to go to sleep. Sometimes I miss those days," Norman told him. He then suddenly looked at the portrait and then back at Trevor again.

"Is there something wrong, sir?" inquired Trevor. "No, my dear child, nothing. I think that I see the trunk. It's there, near my boxes of vinyls and old record player," Norman answered. Once they got the photo album out of the attic, they went back downstairs. Surprisingly, Birdie had finished paying all the bills, and she was now in the room where Trevor had been playing chess with Margaret. They were talking and laughing about something.

"What's so funny, you two?" asked Norman. "We were just reminiscing about the time that we all went to the beach when Margaret and I were little and that boy knocked down our sandcastle and made us cry. We got back at him by throwing his clothes into the ocean and, while we were swimming, saw them floating there. It was so gratifying for us," Rhonda replied. "I'm glad that you have such fond memories of your childhood and all of the good times that there were," Norman began.

"What do you have there, Uncle?" inquired Margaret.

"I was able to locate an old family photo album with Trevor's help and thought we could look through it all together when we get back," Norman answered.

"Are we going somewhere, sir?" inquired Trevor.

"Yes, I was talking to my travel agent and was able to book reservations at a hotel in Key West. Since we've known each other for a long time, he was able to give me a discount, so I would pay less than it would really cost. In other words, we're going on a vacation," Norman replied.

"Oh, Uncle, that's so great! It's been a long time since we've gone away, and it's very much overdue," Birdie said excitedly.

"How many days are we going for?" asked Margaret.

"Only one, but that will be enough time to see everything that there is to see and also have some time to rest and relax before we come back. So all of you go upstairs and start packing what you will need," Norman answered.

"Sir, I've never been on a vacation before and don't know what I should pack," Trevor told him.

"There's no need to worry about that. Either Margaret or Rhonda will help you once they're finished packing for themselves," Norman added.

It didn't take long for everyone to pack. Margaret helped Trevor, and they got into the car and were on their way. Along the way, Trevor read every sign that he saw and observed every bit of scenery that he could. They only made one stop at a gas station in Key Largo to get gas and some snacks to hold them over until dinner since they didn't eat lunch. Then, they started again toward their destination.

When they arrived in Key West, the first thing that they did was check into their hotel and put their luggage in their rooms. Trevor and Norman had a room together that had two separate beds, and next door to them was Margaret and Birdie's room.

After that, they went to downtown Key West and walked around Duval Street, which had a lot of different things to do. Because there were a lot of people walking the streets, Trevor stayed as close to Norman as he could. They first went to the southernmost point in the continental United States, which is a famous tourist attraction and historical landmark.

"What do you think?" Norman asked Trevor.

"It's truly amazing, sir. I never knew that such a monument ever existed, but now that I do, I'm exuberant just looking at it," Trevor replied.

Since they had arrived in Key West so late, it was around dinnertime, and they found a place to get a bite to eat. After that, they decided to walk some more and went to Sunset Celebration at Mallory Square, where there were all kinds of attractions and entertainment, such as street performers. They watched a show of a man who was a sword swallower and who demonstrated this unique talent to a whole crowd of people.

"Isn't that something?" asked Norman.

"Yes, sir. I would say it is. I have never witnessed anyone who could do a thing like that. It's incredible," Trevor replied.

"Maybe we should head back to the car and call it a day. Tomorrow we can sightsee some more before going back home," Margaret began.

"Yes, all this walking has tired me out, and I need rest and to get a good night's sleep. It's also almost Trevor's bedtime anyway," Birdie said.

So they walked back to their car. Along the way, there was a scruffy-looking man sitting on a folding chair, with a glass jar on the floor beside him, and on the other side was a bottle of alcohol. He was holding up a cardboard sign that said, "Dirty jokes for twenty dollars."

As they passed the scruffy-looking man, Trevor became curious. "What do dirty jokes mean?" he inquired.

"It's something that children should never know about until they grow up. People like that man rip others off with pointless things that they think will make them a lot of money," Norman answered.

When they got back to the hotel, Trevor got into his pajamas and then hopped into bed. He watched an animated movie that was on television but fell asleep during it. Norman went next door to say "Good night" to his nieces and was about to go back to his room but didn't and stayed to keep Margaret and Rhonda company for a little bit before he too went to sleep. Norman wanted to tell his nieces about Trevor and the portrait that was in the attic but decided to wait until they got back home to discuss it because it wasn't the time or place for that. They wanted to enjoy what was left of their vacation on Key West.

"Is Trevor asleep yet?" asked Margaret.

"Yes, he is. I will go back to my room to go check on him soon," Norman replied. "I have to say that key lime pie that I had for dessert was so good and was like the way that our mother made it. She was a very talented cook and baker," Birdie told them.

"That's where we learned it all from. If it wasn't for her, we wouldn't know how to prepare anything. She was such a good teacher who was very patient with us," rejoined Margaret.

"I've been thinking about something, and it has to do with Trevor's well-being," Norman began. "I would say that he's in a loving home with people who care deeply about him. There's not much more a child like him could want," Rhonda said.

"I am not talking about that. I mean from the account he gave us when we first met him makes me feel sorry for him to have put up with such a bad batch, and it all started with that horrendous church that he was born in. Places like that should be shut down permanently," Norman replied.

"If I remember right, he also fell into the wrong crowd, as well, but that wasn't his fault because he didn't know any better at that time," Margaret added.

"I believe you're referring to those horrific street people. They'll get what's coming to them someday, and when that happens, Trevor will be the one who has the last laugh," Norman told them.

"What about that man named Swindle?" asked Birdie. "He seems just as wicked as the others. There's also the other man with the spider tattoo. We need to figure out how all of them are connected and make sure that they're no longer at large and can't harm Trevor ever again," Margaret began.

"I'll take care of that, and if I have to hire a private detective to aid me in uncovering what these atrocious people's purpose is for trying to hurt Trevor, they must have some cause for it, and I'm going to find out what that is," Norman said.

"But we don't know much about them other than what Trevor has told us. They must be stopped at all costs and never be allowed to misuse anyone else for their vile and underhanded schemes ever again," Rhonda replied.

"What I don't get is how they found our home. It's not like they knew where it is that Trevor was, and they would have had to ascertain that kind of knowledge from another person or third party," Margaret added.

"Who do you think it was?" asked Birdie.

"Knowing them, it was most likely one of their own who might have been sent to purposely spy on and follow us. That shows just how low these people will stoop just to regain Trevor," Norman told them.

"Don't you think you're being a little paranoid, Uncle?" inquired Margaret.

"No, not in the least bit. From what we already know, their objective is to get Trevor back and hurt him in some way, and now that they know where we live, that could pose an even bigger problem for us. Making sure that Trevor doesn't fall into the wrong hands again is crucial," Norman replied.

"We won't let that happen. I think it's a good idea that one of us stays in the room with Trevor just in case they show up again. Then we can call the police. That's the smart thing to do because there's a good chance that they will break in, and if that occurs, we could be in just as much danger," Rhonda began.

"What if I were to be the one who protects Trevor from them?" inquired Norman.

"That wouldn't be a very smart idea. They could be carrying weapons and might use them on you. That's what the police are for. They'll keep all of us safe, and that gives me peace of mind," Margaret answered.

"I'm not so sure about that. While it's their job to protect people like us, if we were to call them, it could take them a while to arrive. And by then, it would be too late. We can't wait for the police to show up when we're in a dire situation that could cost us our lives. These people aren't to be underestimated in any way," Norman began.

"It's getting late, and we should all be going to sleep now. We'll see each other in the morning. I saw when we checked in that this hotel has a free continental buffet for its guests. We can do that, then go sightseeing some more for a little bit," Birdie said.

They then said "Good night" to one another and went to sleep. Trevor was still asleep, lying very still. It took Norman a little more time for him to fall asleep. He couldn't get out of his head the uncanny resemblance that Trevor had to his sister Grace. As far as he knew, she never had any children of her own, or at least that was Norman thought. If what he believed was true and that Trevor was, in fact, his sister's child, then that would make Norman Trevor's grandfather. But it wasn't likely because even if Grace did keep Trevor a secret from him, she would have wanted him to know eventually. But then again, maybe not. Grace was the kind of person who kept all kinds of secrets and lied constantly. But despite all that, the one thing that Norman was angry about was that she kept Trevor from him for such a long time. If he had known that he had a grandson, Norman would have done something sooner to help Trevor avoid his heinous past. After a little while of lying awake and thinking, Norman was able to clear his mind and fall asleep. He knew that when they got home, he might have to tell his nieces, but Norman would cross that bridge when he got there. Until then, he was going to enjoy the remainder of the trip with the people he was most fond of.

CHAPTER 2

An Unusual Interview, Which Is Also the Sequel to the Previous Chapter

Trevor was having the time of his life while vacationing in Key West. He had seen and experienced things that he never would have thought possible. It was all new and exciting to him, something he would remember for the rest of his life. Trevor couldn't wait to see what else there was to do while he was in Key West. However, they were only staying until the early afternoon to avoid traffic on the way home. This shortened their time, but it didn't matter to them. Trevor had gotten his first taste of a place he wished he never had to leave.

The next day, when everyone had awakened, they had their breakfast. Then there was a change of plans. Instead of exploring more of Key West, they decided to stay at the hotel, which had a pool. Margaret and Rhonda wanted to lounge by the pool, even though there was no sun.

"I wish I knew how to swim. The pool water looks very refreshing," Trevor began.

"That's something we can teach you if you really want to learn. I had a job as a lifeguard one summer when I was a teenager and also taught children lessons on how to swim," Margaret said.

"When was that?" asked Birdie.

"You were young and wouldn't remember, but she made one heck of a lifeguard and was a good swimming instructor, as well. I remember I had to sometimes pick her up, and the children begged her not to leave them," Norman answered.

"Can I just sit and put my feet in the water?" inquired Trevor.

"Of course, you can. But just as long as you don't go any further than that, we'll keep an eye on you from here," Rhonda replied.

So Trevor sat and soaked his feet in the water. It felt good to him. After they were done at the pool, they checked out of the hotel and started on their journey back home. The trip felt longer than it did when they were going, but Trevor practiced his reading and was able to finish a few chapters of *The Swiss Family Robinson* to help pass the time.

When they finally got home, they unpacked all their stuff. Suddenly the phone rang, and Rhonda answered it.

"Who is on the phone?" asked Norman.

"It's your friend Mr. Greenfield. He was wondering if he could come over for a visit because he also wants to hear all about our trip," Birdie replied.

"Tell him that it's alright and to give me ten minutes to finish unpacking, then I will call him to come over," Norman said.

Once they were all done unpacking, Norman called Mr. Greenfield back to tell him to come over because he only lived a few minutes away. Soon enough, there was a knock at the door, and Margaret answered it.

"Hello there, Mr. Greenfield. What an unexpected pleasure it is to see you. My uncle is in his office, waiting for you," Margaret said.

"Good, because I wasn't sure if he was up to having anyone over after you just got home from your trip and all, but he said that there was something that he needed to talk to me about, so here I am," Mr. Greenfield replied. He went in and followed Margaret to Norman's office.

"Uncle, your friend Mr. Greenfield is here to see you," Margaret added.

"You're just in time, my friend. Silly me, I almost forgot. Margaret, please go get your sister for me because I need to talk to the two of you, as well," Norman told her.

Margaret went to find Rhonda, who was in the living room with Trevor. When they went back, Norman instructed them to close the door so they could talk without being heard.

"Why did you call us all here, Norman?" inquired Mr. Greenfield.

"There is something that you all should know. It may be shocking, but I don't know for sure if it's true or not," Norman answered.

"Uncle," asked Margaret, "what are you trying to tell us?"

"Before we left to go on our trip to Key West, I was in the attic with Trevor, looking for the photo album, and we came across a portrait of my younger sister Grace. This may sound absurd, but I noticed a resemblance in both of them, and I think that Trevor may be my grandson," Norman replied.

"That can't be. If he was, I assume that your sister would have told you," Birdie began.

"Not necessarily. Aunt Grace, from what I remember of her, didn't like to share personal things with anyone. She apparently had a lot of secrets but chose never to tell anyone about them. It was kind of strange," Margaret said.

"I still say that boy isn't to be trusted and needs to be watched at all times because he's a rotten little child that takes everything and runs. I'll eat my words if not," Mr. Greenfield replied.

"Come now, Victor. Can't you at least try and change the way you think about Trevor? He's not a bad child. He just has had some hard times, and that doesn't mean that he's anything like those people he was once around. It shows that they weren't able to corrupt his mind to make him the way they are," Norman added.

"How are we to know for sure?" asked Margaret.

"There is no way unless we can do some research about the boy's family history, and that should tell us if you're right or not," Mr. Greenfield answered.

"Uncle, you did do just that. Remember the paper that you printed out? That might be what we need to know for certain," Rhonda told them.

"Yes, that's true, but I misplaced it and can't seem to remember the name of the website that I used to find out the information from. I will have to look for it. But what I have told you must stay between us, and Trevor must not know until I think he is ready, because it might be too much for him to handle," Norman began.

"If what you say is true and the boy truly is your grandson, then it wouldn't surprise me in the least bit. I remember your sister very well, and she always kept to herself. But something like this, she should have informed you. But that was just how she was, and I found it to be unusual. Don't get me wrong. She was a great person who was loving and caring, but when it came to anything that had to do with her, she wouldn't tell a soul," Mr. Greenfield said.

"I need some more time to think this over. We can regroup and revisit it in, let's say, two weeks from now. But I need one of you to go back into the living room and check on Trevor. And if you ladies don't mind, I would like to be alone with my friend for the rest of the visit." Norman replied.

"We completely understand, Uncle, and will leave the two of you to talk amongst yourselves," Margaret added. She and Birdie then got up and went out of the office. Rhonda went back into the living room to check on Trevor. He was just sitting on the couch, practicing his writing. "Look, I can spell all of my first name now," Trevor told her, holding up the pad of paper where he had written his first name on it. "That's terrific! The next step is to learn how to spell your last name, which I will teach you today in your lesson," Birdie began. "I also want to learn how to do math problems because I think it's very important. You can also teach me about money, as well," Trevor said.

"Let's focus on one thing at a time because I don't want to overwhelm you with too many things," Rhonda replied. "Is there someone here?" inquired Trevor. "Yes, my uncle's friend Mr. Greenfield came by for a visit, but I think now would be a good time to do your daily lesson since both of us have some free time," Rhonda replied.

"Where can we do it?" asked Trevor. "Here would be okay. You go get your book from upstairs and wait for me. I have to do something, but it won't take that long," Birdie answered. So Trevor went upstairs to his room to get his book, then he went back down and waited for Rhonda. While he was waiting, Trevor practiced reading quietly to himself until Birdie had gone back. The first thing they did was read for a little while, then they switched over to writing. Trevor had only learned to write a few words but managed to write an entire short sentence, which made Rhonda beam with happiness.

After Mr. Greenfield had left, they had a late lunch since they didn't have time to eat when they returned home. After that, Trevor wandered about the house, looking for something to do. He then went back into the kitchen, where Margaret was busy working on what looked like a photo album, gluing different pictures onto it. "What is it that you're doing?" inquired Trevor.

"I'm making a scrapbook of our trip. If you want to, you can help me. I could use the assistance," Margaret replied. "I would like to very much, but I don't know what a scrapbook is or what you do with it," Trevor began.

"That's okay. All you have to do is glue certain pictures onto the pages. I already did a few, so now I will let you do some. Just take the picture, put glue on the back of it, and place it onto the page. But if you need help, just tell me," Margaret said.

"That seems easy enough. I just hope that I don't mess it up by accidentally doing it the wrong way, and that wouldn't be good," Trevor replied.

"It's nothing that you should fret over. Just give it a try. The only thing that I will say is to make sure the picture isn't crooked when you paste it down. It has to be straight. That way, it will look nice," Margaret added.

"Alright then, here goes nothing," Trevor told her. He picked up one of the pictures, put glue on the back of it, and pasted it straight onto the page, right underneath another one of the pictures that Margaret had already done.

"How was that?" asked Trevor.

"Perfect! Now we only have a few more left, then it will be done, and we can show it to my uncle and Birdie. They don't know that I was putting together a scrapbook, but they will be very elated to see that I made something to commemorate our trip together," Margaret began.

"I think so too. If you wouldn't mind, I'd like to do the rest of the pictures because there are only a few more pages left. You already did a lot, so I want to give you a break," Trevor said.

"That's so thoughtful of you. If you really want to finish up the scrapbook, then you have my permission to do so," Margaret replied.

Once they were all finished putting together the scrapbook, Margaret and Trevor gathered everyone together in the living room. "What's this all about?" asked Norman.

"Trevor and I have something that we want to show you that we think you will like a lot. I did the majority of the work, but Trevor helped me a little," Margaret answered.

She then showed them the scrapbook, and they were gleeful at seeing it. They then looked through it together until there was nothing left to see. "That was so great. I really enjoyed it. That was quite the surprise, I must say," Rhonda added.

"Do you, by any chance, want to look at the photo album that was in the attic?" inquired Norman.

"Sure, that would be a lot of fun. I bet there are pictures in there that we can surely reminisce about," Margaret replied.

"Where did you put it, Uncle?" asked Birdie.

"That's a very good question. I know that I had it somewhere in my office before we left for our trip, but I can't think of where I put it," Norman answered.

"It's okay, we'll help you look for it. I'm sure we'll find it, and if not, then it will turn up. But let's see if we can find it," Margaret began.

They then all went out of the living room and into Norman's office. They looked all over for the photo album.

"Did you find it?" inquired Trevor.

"No, but we should keep looking. It's bound to be in here somewhere. Go check over on that chair. There's some stuff on it, maybe it's there," Rhonda replied.

So Trevor went over to the chair and looked through the stuff that was on it but didn't find the photo album—that is, until he saw something at the bottom.

"I think I may have found it," he told them.

Trevor put all the other stuff onto the floor, and sure enough, there was the photo album.

"Nice job. Let's go back into the living room and look through this," Norman added.

So they left the office, went back into the living room, and sat on the couch, slowly looking at every picture that was on the pages.

"I remember this. It was when Birdie and I were twelve, and you had that house in New Hampshire, and we would come visit you every summer, Uncle," Margaret began, pointing to one of the pictures.

"Yes, that house was very strange, if I can remember well. It was built upside down, or so we say. When we were little, we have so many fond memories of that house," Rhonda said.

"Which one is you?" asked Trevor.

"I'm the one on the right. It's funny. When I look at this picture, I don't even recognize myself, but now I do because I remember when it was taken. I do sometimes miss those fun New England summers that we used to have," Margaret replied.

"Yes, I remember when we used to play outside in the sprinklers on the front lawn to cool ourselves off because those days were so hot. That was the only way we could beat the heat," Rhonda added.

"Do you remember the lake that we used to swim in?" asked Margaret.

"Yes, very well. And every Fourth of July, the two of us would sit on the dock in the evenings and watch the fireworks while eating popsicles," Birdie answered.

"Yes, both of you were such adorable children that I can't believe how time went by so fast and you two grew up so quickly. I was there the day both of you were born," Norman told them.

"What's on the next page?" asked Trevor. "This album is in chronological order by year. The picture of Margaret and Rhonda when they were twelve was taken in 1975. Judging from the looks of it, the album goes on for a while. Let's go to the next page and see what's on there," Norman replied.

They then turned to the next page, where there were more photos. "Wow, there sure are a lot more photos on this page than the last one," Trevor began. "Do you remember when this picture was taken?" inquired Birdie.

"Yes, we went to a public park that had a giant lake, and we had a cookout and hung out by the lake for a few hours. I got so badly sunburned that after that, I started using sunscreen when I go out into the sun," Margaret answered.

"What time is it now?" asked Norman.

"It's almost four thirty, Uncle. We still have time before Margaret and I have to start making dinner. We'll start in another hour so that we can eat around six. That's when everything will be ready," Rhonda replied, looking at her watch.

"I think that's enough of taking a trip down memory lane for me. If you all can, continue to look through that album, if you want, but I just remembered that I have to answer a few emails before we eat dinner because the people want an immediate response," Norman said, and he got up from the couch and left the living room.

So Trevor, Margaret, and Birdie kept going through the album until there weren't any more pictures. They ate at six, and after the kitchen was all cleaned up, Trevor found an old jigsaw puzzle in a dresser in his room and tried to put it together himself. But because he had never done anything like that before, he had some help from Margaret, and the two of them were able to put together the puzzle, which was only a hundred pieces.

Until it was time for him to go to sleep, Trevor sat on an armchair and ended up falling asleep before he, too, was about to go upstairs to bed. Norman carried Trevor up to his room and put him into his bed, then went across the way to his room.

During the night, there was a thunderstorm, which scared and woke up Trevor. He fell back to sleep by listening to the sound of the rain falling and the raindrops hitting his window. It was relaxing for him. Even after the thunderstorm was over, it continued to rain throughout the night and didn't stop.

Trevor had nothing but pleasant dreams. It had been a while since he had the recurring nightmare about his past. As he slept comfortably nestled underneath his blanket, Trevor had the most wonderful dream in which he was in the dark and, all of a sudden, there was a white light, and a woman who was dressed all in white took his hand, and the two of them flew over the city together.

Trevor interpreted the woman to be his mother, who had come down from heaven to be with him. While this dream lasted until the morning when Trevor had awoken, he could vaguely remember what had happened in the dream, except that before they departed, the woman smiled at Trevor and disappeared. Whether the woman was his mother, all that Trevor knew was that she was very kind and gentle. He thought about his dream the entire day and hoped that when he went to sleep, he would dream of the kind woman in white again.

CHAPTER 3

Describes a Shocking Secret about Trevor's Past, as Narrated by Spyder to Pastor Swanson and His Wife

On a rainy Tuesday night, there was more traffic on the road than was usual. It was bumper to bumper all the way, especially on the highway heading south. While there hadn't been any accidents reported yet, it was because of the torrential rain that was slowing everyone down. People were getting very impatient and honking their horns like mad. There was no way around it. The traffic did, however, start to move a little bit, but it would be a while before it subsided completely, which made it worse.

Among the people who were caught in the traffic were Pastor Swanson and his wife. They were on their way down to Miami for a meeting with Spyder. This was because he sent Pastor Swanson an email a few days prior and didn't give much detail, except for him and his wife to meet him at an abandoned old warehouse near Biscayne Bay, and that was all. Pastor Swanson had told his wife about the email that he received and that they had to go down to Miami that same night and nothing further. This whole thing was shrouded in mystery to the pastor's wife, who agreed to do it only under the condition that she would be made a part of whatever he was doing. But unknown to her, that was the way that her husband had planned it all along.

"I still don't see why we have to go down to Miami," the pastor's wife began. "There's a good reason for it, and you will find out when we get there, that is, if we can ever get out of this traffic and make it there on time," Pastor Swanson said.

"I don't like this one bit. Miami is a place that has a lot of dangerous and malicious people lurking all around. It's no place for a pastor or his wife to be wandering about the streets, especially at this time of night," the pastor's wife replied.

"Why must you always worry about things that might not happen?" asked Pastor Swanson.

"It's a matter of safety, that's why. If we get mugged, I hope you're prepared to do something about it. Otherwise, we'll both end up laying dead in a puddle of our own blood, then you'll be sorry that you ever dragged me to ever agree to this," the pastor's wife answered.

"Don't be like that, honey. I promise you, this isn't for nothing, and I will pay a lot once everything is finally done," Pastor Swanson added.

"I hope you're right because if not, you'll be sleeping on the couch for a while until I say you don't have to anymore. That was part of the agreement, remember?" the pastor's wife told him.

"Yes, I am aware of that. The only thing that we have to do is give some information, and then we can be on our way back home. It shouldn't take too long," Pastor Swanson began.

"Who is this man we're meeting?" inquired the pastor's wife.

"He's someone that I am doing some business with. I don't know much about him. He just came to the church one day and demanded to talk to me, so that's what we did. It was a spur-of-the-moment thing that I had no choice but to take care of because he claimed it was very important. Oh, look, the traffic is getting better. We should be there in no time," Pastor Swanson replied.

"Something tells me that this whole thing is some kind of scam that you got yourself into without realizing what might happen. If that's the case, then we're going to have a long and serious talk on the way home about not falling for people's trickery so easily," the pastor's wife said.

"I can assure you it's not like that. This man is not a fraud. He's someone that I know won't use us just to get what he wants. We made a deal with each other and agreed to stick to it. So just let me do all of the talking. But if you want to chime in on something, then I have no objection to that," Pastor Swanson replied.

"How do you know that he's not some kind of crook?" asked the pastor's wife.

"Well, for one thing, he doesn't seem like the kind of person who would promise something then stiff us on purpose," Pastor Swanson answered.

"I still think this whole thing is a bad idea, but that's just my opinion. And to think that I could be getting ready to go to sleep now, but instead, I am taking a road trip with you to a place that I feel uneasy about going to," the pastor's wife added.

"Why is it that you want to go to sleep so badly for?" inquired Pastor Swanson.

"If you must know, I need my beauty sleep so that I am in a good mood the next day. If I don't get any sleep, I become irritable and unpleasant, and that's a side of me that you don't want to see very often because it's not pretty," the pastor's wife replied.

When they finally made it to Miami, they parked their car and walked around trying to find the abandoned warehouse that Spyder had mentioned in his email. "Where is this place anyway?" asked the pastor's wife.

"I don't really know. He didn't give any directions to the location where we're supposed to go, but it should be around here somewhere," Pastor Swanson answered.

Just then, they heard a metal door opening, and they looked to see the abandoned warehouse they had been looking for. They hurried toward it to get out of the rain, even though they had an umbrella and were sharing it, but that didn't stop them from getting a little wet. When they got inside the warehouse, it was completely dark, and there was no sign of Spyder anywhere. However, they could hear strange noises from afar. "Where is the man that we're supposed to meet with?" inquired the pastor's wife.

"I assume that he's in here, but since it's dark, we're not able to see him. Maybe if I yell something, he will respond back," Pastor Swanson replied.

He then yelled out something that echoed throughout the entire warehouse, but there was no response. All of a sudden, a thunderstorm started outside. There was thunder and lightning. Through the light that the lightning provided, they saw someone standing in front of them. "It's one of those ruffians who wants to take our money! Stand up to him," the pastor's wife began, hiding behind her husband. There was again thunder and lightning. It was at that point that Pastor Swanson realized the person in front of them was Spyder.

"I didn't think you would show, but I guess I was wrong. There's an old office over there. That's where we'll talk," he said. They walked across the warehouse to the old office. Both Pastor Swanson and his wife sat down, as did Spyder, who sat down at the desk. "What's this all about?" asked the pastor's wife.

"I'm surprised you didn't tell her. She is your wife, after all. And I told you not to keep it a secret from her because she's now involved in this too," Spyder answered.

"I was going to, but I felt like she should find out about this on her own instead of hearing it through me. If I were to have done that, she might have agreed to come with me tonight, and I could come with her," Pastor Swanson added.

"Well, since she's in the dark about all of this, it's my duty to explain the purpose of what it is that we're going to do and why," Spyder told him. "What's he talking about?" inquired the pastor's wife.

"There's a reason behind all of this, but I will let him tell you since this whole thing was his idea. I just felt by going along with it, it would help us in some ways, especially when it comes to money," Pastor Swanson began. "Alright then, you've got my full attention. Now, enlighten me on what this has to do with me and how much money I'm going to get," the pastor's wife said.

"All in good time, my dear lady. I must explain to you the main reason why we're all teaming up. A few years ago, there was a boy who was born in your church. His name is Trevor Conway. I know what you're thinking, what do I want with him? Well, I'm his cousin, and on the day of his birth, his mother lost something that I need back so that he isn't ever to discover his real identity," Spyder replied.

"I don't know what you're referring to. I know nothing of that. Yes, he was born in our church, but whatever it is that you're trying to reclaim, we don't have it," the pastor's wife added. "You wretched woman, stop lying to me. I know one of you must have it. Now, hand it over, and if you keep refusing, then I'll take it by force," Spyder told her. "Say that again if you dare. Go on and see what happens."

The pastor's wife stood up, her demeanor calm. "Let's all try to stay composed and work together," she said as she glanced at Pastor Swanson, who nodded. "What was said isn't worth getting upset over," he added reassuringly before she settled back into her seat.

"Are you going to give me what I want or not?" inquired Spyder, his tone impatient.

"For the last time, we don't have anything that belonged to that boy's mother," the pastor's wife replied firmly. "She had nothing on her when she came to our church."

"What exactly is it?" asked Pastor Swanson, his curiosity piqued.

"A gold wedding ring. It belonged to his mother," Spyder explained, pointing at the pastor's wife. "She had it on her finger that night, and someone took it. I believe that person was you."

"It wasn't me. I knew nothing about it. The one who had it was an old woman named Joan. She stole the ring and kept it for a long time without telling anyone until the day she died a few weeks ago.

After that, I don't know what happened to it," the pastor's wife added defensively.

"I can tell you're not telling the truth. When Joan died, you were the one who took it and have it with you right now," Spyder accused.

"How do you know that?" inquired the pastor's wife, feeling uneasy.

"I can see there's something small in your pocket. There's no hiding it from me anymore. I need that ring, and you will give it to me, or else," Spyder insisted.

"Don't make ultimatums to us. We're just people who work in a church and don't know anything about a wedding ring. If we did, we'd gladly give it to you," Pastor Swanson interjected calmly.

"Okay, I'll come clean. You're right. I do have the ring. I took it when Joan died, but only because she told me everything, and I couldn't just get rid of the ring. It's worthless to me now, so you can have it," the pastor's wife admitted reluctantly. She then retrieved the wedding ring from her pocket and handed it to Spyder, whose eyes widened with glee.

"I finally have it. Now, all I need to do is get rid of it for good, and then there will only be a few more things that have to be done before we can triumph," Spyder declared triumphantly.

"How do you plan to dispose of it?" asked Pastor Swanson, intrigued.

"That's something I haven't thought much about. But first, I need you to tell me more information about the boy, and it has to be entirely truthful," Spyder requested. "He was in your care for some time. If you could give me a short summary of what it was like when he was in your care?"

"As you already know, the boy was born and raised in our church. He, at one time, attended our training program for children but managed to cause trouble," Pastor Swanson told him.

"What kind of trouble?" asked Spyder.

"He flat out refused to follow the rules, and there was an incident that caused him to get thrown out of the training program, and I think that he may have stolen some money from me, as well," Pastor Swanson replied.

"What was done about it?" inquired Spyder.

"Our board of directors decided to try to place him elsewhere. We found somewhere, a foster home, but he continued to start trouble with the other children. He ran away late at night. Most of the time when Trevor was with us, he was kept away from the other children, but we took a chance putting him in the training program not knowing what would happen. We hoped that it would work out, but Trevor never wanted to listen or follow the rules. He turned out to be more trouble than we could handle," Pastor Swanson replied.

"How did you know that he ran away from the foster home?" asked Spyder.

"One of the people who run the program called us up the next day and told us they looked all over the house but couldn't find him," Pastor Swanson replied.

"I can tell you that a child like Trevor does come around every once in a while, but most of the time, all of the children are very well behaved. And if any of them were to act out, we would do something on the spot so that there isn't any chaos in our church. We believe that children should be seen and not heard," the pastor's wife began.

"What was your relationship with the boy?" inquired Spyder.

"If you must know, he was my apprentice for a short time before he went into the training program. I will admit that I spoiled him too much, but I only did it because I felt like he needed a parental figure in his life. But the church has very strict rules against something like that, and at the time, I didn't think anybody would ever find out," the pastor's wife answered.

"Do you plan to give us money?" asked Pastor Swanson.

"Yes, I think you gave me enough information that you both should be rewarded with something," Spyder replied, and he pulled out two one-hundred-dollar bills from his wallet and gave them to Pastor Swanson and his wife, who put them away quickly.

"We should get going now because we have a long drive back home and need to get some sleep. It was nice seeing you again," Pastor Swanson said, and he and his wife stood up as if they were about to leave.

"Sit down. We're not finished here yet. I still have to tell you my side of the story, so your sleep will just have to wait," Spyder replied, and both Pastor Swanson and his wife sat back down again.

"You can't keep us here all night, you know. We have to get some sleep because we have work tomorrow," Pastor Swanson added.

"How long do you expect for us to stay here?" inquired the pastor's wife.

"Once you hear what I have to say, then you will be free to go. But until then, you will listen to what I have to say," Spyder told them.

"Is there any way that you can be brief?" asked Pastor Swanson.

"No, I must tell you what I need to tell you. The boy's mother is my third cousin once removed. She got married to a man, and on their wedding day, he gave her that ring. It has something engraved in it. His parents made out a will before they died, left everything, such as a lot of money and that ring, as well. I was the one who was going to inherit the family fortune, but that was before the boy was born. After he was, they changed the will to make him the next in line instead of me," Spyder replied.

"I still don't see what that has to do with us," the pastor's wife began.

"The old dame who worked in your church had the ring, then you did. It's imperative that the boy never gets the money from the will or the ring. That's why I called you two here tonight. Because as my partners, you will help me make sure that the boy doesn't inherit anything from his parents' will. Now let's go outside for a second. There's something that I must do," Spyder said.

They all got up and went out of the warehouse onto a dock down a ladder, ending up right near the Biscayne Bay.

"Why are we here?" asked Pastor Swanson.

"Like I told you before, I must see to it that the boy never discovers his true identity, and the only way he could do that is through one thing, and you already know what it is," Spyder answered.

He then pulled out the gold wedding ring from his pocket and threw it into Biscayne Bay. Both Pastor Swanson and his wife looked mortified at what they just witnessed.

"You two can go now, but I will contact you again soon. You must tell no one about this meeting or about the ring because we can't have any kind of word getting out about this," Spyder told them.

Pastor Swanson and his wife drove him in complete silence. They couldn't believe all that was revealed to them, especially about the ring. They were more interested in gaining the money for themselves than anything else. Pastor Swanson was not happy that his wife had kept the ring a secret from him the entire time, but that didn't matter anymore because the ring was now at the bottom of Biscayne Bay, and Trevor's true identity couldn't be discovered by anyone. While the ring may have been lost forever, that wasn't going to stop Norman from finding out whether Trevor was his grandson. But with this dastardly plot in the works, that meant that there was going to be a lot more trouble ahead for Trevor because now that everyone whom Spyder had handpicked to aid him was now all on board, this became more crucial than ever.

CHAPTER 4

Gives in Greater Detail Another Conspiracy Created by Three Sinister Foes That the Reader Is Already Acquainted with and the Proclamation Made to Mr. Albert Swindle by Spyder

Now that June was no more and the next month had already come, it was no secret that summer was already halfway over. Soon enough, the next season would be here before we knew it, even though it wasn't that far away. As summer was slowly starting to die down, there was more of it to still go around, but it would soon be on its way out for good and become just a memory, especially when fall officially kicked in.

While people were trying to make the most of what was left of the current season by getting out into the fresh air as much as they could, it was impossible because of the unpredictable weather conditions. However, this didn't stop some from still going about their daily lives and being brave enough to brace any storm.

Spyder stayed in Miami for a few more days after he had met with Pastor Swanson and his wife, and then he headed north to Fort Lauderdale. It was lucky for him that Mr. Albert Swindle happened to be in the same city because after going a long time without doing a show, he finally caught a break and was asked to perform for a children's birthday party. Spyder contacted Mr. Swindle so that they could meet up somewhere.

Before he left Miami, Spyder went to see Brock Ferguson again and invited him and his associates to join him at the same pub where he had first met Mr. Albert Swindle and where they had conceived their brilliant plan together. They all agreed to meet up on Saturday after Mr. Swindle was finished with his show, which would be sometime in the late afternoon.

While he had some free time before the meet up, Spyder went around the city, seeing different things, and stopped to get something to eat on east Las Olas Boulevard. Then, he went to the pub to wait for the others. When he got there, Spyder sat at the bar, where music was playing from the jukebox.

"Do you need a refill?" asked Zeke.

"No, I'm actually waiting for some people, and I'll have another drink once they arrive, but for now, leave me be," Spyder answered.

"Alright, but if you need another drink, let me know," the African American bartender said as he walked away.

After waiting for an hour, Mr. Albert Swindle was the first to show up. He spotted Spyder and went over to him.

"It's good to see you again. I hope you have been well. In case you're wondering, the show at the birthday party didn't do so well. The children all booed me and threw stuff at me. Then some of the parents blamed me for the whole thing and said that they would never use me ever again. The one time I get a lucky break, it goes awry. Some people have all of the luck," Mr. Swindle said.

"That's too bad. I thought that the rain would have slowed you down and you might have shown up here late. But it looks like you survived putting up with the little ones, even if they did find your act uninteresting. They're all unruly little brats anyway," Spyder replied.

"Is this seat taken?" inquired Albert Swindle. "I was hoping that we can get a table so that we all can be together, but from the looks of it, there's none available right now," Spyder added.

"I see a big one over there that would be perfect for us. Let's go claim it before someone else does," Mr. Swindle told him, and the two of them hurried over to a big table and sat down.

"Did it take you long to get here?" asked Spyder.

"No, I was actually in the area. After the party, I went to a pawnshop to see if I could sell a few of my things to get some money. The owner wasn't interested in any of what I was trying to sell him, so afterwards, I came right here," Mr. Swindle replied.

Just then, Mr. Ferguson walked in along with Red, Stranger, Lola, Doc, and Abigail. They sat down at the table.

"Why did you call us all here for?" inquired Brock.

"I have called this meet up to discuss some important matters. But first, I must bring some of you up to speed on the other part of my plan, which is to kidnap the boy and get him to come back to us," Spyder replied.

"How do you plan to make that happen?" asked Mr. Ferguson.

"We wait until the time is right. Then, when no one is around, we get him. But we have to decide on who is going to assist me in doing that," Spyder answered.

"You do realize that he never goes anywhere alone. Therefore, it would be impossible for us to do something like that and not get caught," Abigail began.

"My dear girl, you are so young and yet so naive. We already know where he is. It's just a matter of being able to get him. Then, once we have the boy, those people who he's with will never be able to find him," Albert Swindle said.

"How do we decide on who is going to do this?" inquired Doc.

"Mr. Spyder and I have talked it over and think that the first person who we chose that we feel would be perfect is Lola because she's very cunning and sharp-witted," Mr. Swindle replied.

"What do I have to do?" asked Lola.

"All you have to do is do what we tell you to, and that goes for the rest of you because we can't have anyone who is just going to get in the way," Brock answered.

"I think I'll pass on it, and you should pick somebody else. I don't want to have a hand in something like kidnapping," Lola added.

"Who else do you suggest?" inquired Albert Swindle.

"I think that Stranger should go because he would do it easily and without leaving a trace. I nominate him," Mr. Ferguson replied.

"Sorry, I can't do it because I already have a criminal record, and I don't need any more felonies or misdemeanors. I can't risk breaking the law again and getting thrown in jail," Red Stranger told them.

"Fine, then at least I need you to do some spying on the boy, and Doc will go with you. We already know where he is, but we need two people to scout out the place. That will be both of your jobs," Swindle said. "Swindle already has that boy, who is employed by him, into this, as well. He will lure Trevor in, but he needs another person," Brock added.

All then looked at Abigail, who didn't know why they were all staring at her. "Don't look at me. I don't want to be included in this because I think we should just forget the whole thing and leave the boy alone," she replied.

"It's not an option or up for debate. Otherwise, you'll get a beating you'll never forget," Mr. Ferguson added.

"Why should I be the one to do it?" asked Abigail.

"My dear girl, you must understand something. We need to get that boy back because he might have said something that could be bad for all of us, including you. That's why you have to help us because if you do, it won't go unnoticed, if you know what I mean," Mr. Swindle answered.

"You will all receive a little something once the boy is back with us, but not until then. It's a matter that concerns all of us, and we need to work as a team to make sure it happens," Spyder began.

"Bribing me won't change my answer. I can't take part in this, nor do I want to, and that's final," Abigail said.

"Don't give us any of your attitude, girl. You know what will happen if you don't, so make the right decision," Brock replied.

"Why are you being so stubborn for?" inquired Albert Swindle.

"I'm not. To me, it's just pointless to get Trevor back when it would be easy for the police to find him. But that's beside the point," Abigail replied.

"What do you want to do, Abby?" asked Mr. Ferguson.

"Alright, then I'll do it, but don't ask me to do anything like this ever again because I already have a bad feeling that it's not going to work," Abigail answered.

"We don't need any negativity from you, girl. We're in this together, and no matter the outcome, we have to persevere. There's no other way," Brock told them.

"When are we to do this?" inquired Red Stranger.

"That is to be determined by Mr. Ferguson and myself. We will continue to plan this some more and inform you all when the time comes," Mr. Swindle replied.

"How is no one going to know where we are?" inquired Doc.

"We are going to go somewhere that no one will ever think to look for us, and not even the police know about it. If everything goes the way it should, then there's no way that anyone would be able to figure out our location," Mr. Ferguson answered.

"Where is that?" asked Red Stranger. "All will be revealed in time. The two of us already have a place that we think would be ideal to go to, and as long as we aren't seen by anyone else, everything will run smoothly, and the boy will once again be with us," Albert Swindle replied.

"What do you plan to do with him once we have him?" inquired Abigail. "We haven't really thought about that, but we just have to get him back first and then decide that later on," Brock answered.

"How do you plan to lure the boy in so easily?" asked Lola. "My boy Nathan will be the bait, and while he's doing that, Abigail will cause a distraction so that no one suspects any foul play," Mr. Swindle answered.

"Are you going to give me anything?" asked Brock. "Of course, but it has to be the same amount that I give the others because I'm getting low on money and can't afford to pay a lot. Because that show didn't go as I planned it to, I can only pay evenly," Albert Swindle replied.

"Don't cheat me, Swindle, because if you do, then you can forget this whole partnership and you can get the boy back on your own. I need the money more than any of them," Mr. Ferguson began. "Don't worry, I plan to pay you what I said I would, and I'm a man of my word. This partnership won't be in vain. That I can honestly say. And now we have everything that we need to pull it off," Spyder said.

"I'll get Stranger and Doc on it right away to stake out the area, and while they do that, no one is to do anything further until either myself, Mr. Spyder, or Mr. Swindle say to," Brock replied.

"Where do we have to go?" inquired Red Stranger.

"I will give you the address of where the boy is. You must be inconspicuous as much as possible so that no one gets suspicious," Albert Swindle answered.

"How are we going to get there?" asked Doc.

"You can take a public bus. There's one that goes from here to where you need to go. The fare is very expensive, but here's some extra money to get you there and back. I'm warning you two now, don't use it for anything else because if I find out that you did, you'll answer to me," Spyder replied, and he pulled out a whole handful of money and gave it to them, which they put away quickly.

"What do you want me to do?" inquired Abigail.

"My dear girl, you have the most important job of them all and have to start preparing right away. We will brief you on what your task is, but for now, you are to practice and memorize what we tell you to," Mr. Swindle answered.

Just then, the music playing on the jukebox turned off, and a man began playing guitar and singing. This amused Red, Stranger, Doc, and Lola, but not Mr. Ferguson or Mr. Swindle. Spyder found it to be a nuisance, and they both covered their ears to block out the sound.

"Do you want to go to a quieter part of the pub?" asked Albert Swindle.

"Yes, please. I can't take all of this noise. It's assaulting my ears," Brock replied.

All three men moved to the other side of the pub, where it was much quieter, so they could talk some more without the disturbance.

"Should we get a drink at the bar?" inquired Lola.

"No, you can. I'm not really thirsty and was going to go sit at a different table to do some thinking," Abigail answered. She got up and walked over to another table and sat there alone, lost in deep thought, while Lola went up to the bar to get a drink and then came back to where she had been sitting before to listen to the music.

"Do you really think that this plan of yours will work?" asked Spyder.

"Of course, it will, just as long as we execute it perfectly and don't do anything to draw attention to ourselves," Mr. Swindle replied.

"What if it doesn't?" inquired Mr. Ferguson.

"I came up with a plan B just in case, which is we all retreat and go in different directions so that it would be hard to find all of us, and we meet somewhere that is secluded," Albert Swindle answered.

"That's pure genius. With all of us scattered all over the place, it would make it harder for the police to find all of us. We just need a place to meet," Brock began.

"No, you fools! That defeats the whole purpose of what we're trying to do. We can't take any chances. We must get the boy back first, then we'll decide from there," Spyder said.

"You make a valid point. We need to all stay together. Once we have the boy back, then we hit the road and get as far away from the people who have been taking care of him as we can. With no way of knowing it was us, we'll be in the clear. It can't go wrong," Mr. Swindle replied.

"Where do we plan to meet?" inquired Mr. Ferguson.

"I was thinking the liquor store where you all hang out. If we go to the place that you usually are, then no one will be able to see us or know what we're doing," Spyder answered.

"I like that idea because the back of the store is hidden, so there's no way people can rat us out to the police," Albert Swindle added.

"What about that boy of yours, Swindle?" asked Spyder.

"He's loyal to me and will make the perfect bait to lure Trevor in. When they reunite with each other, my thought is that Trevor will be glad to see him again and, because of it, will be completely voluble, leaving us to set the rest of the trap. And in no time at all, we'll have him back with us. But everything has to go swimmingly in order to work out in our favor," Mr. Swindle replied.

"Do you think he'll come quietly?" inquired Brock.

"I would imagine not. He will most likely try to resist, get away, and scream for help. One of you is going to have to keep him from escaping and quiet until we can get away safely in Swindle's caravan. But it can't hold all of us, so only a few people can go while the others do something else," Spyder answered.

"Are you coming with us?" asked Albert Swindle.

"No, I have some other business to attend to, but I will meet you in the back of the liquor store. You all will have to figure out who's going in Swindle's caravan amongst yourselves," Spyder replied.

"Well, I know already that we could use the help of both Stranger and Doc. That only leaves me, because Abigail has a different assignment but needs to go with us. I think that's plenty of people. Now we should get going because it looks like it's going to start raining again any minute," Mr. Ferguson told them.

He then got up to round up the rest of his associates, who all obeyed. The only one left was Abigail, who was still sitting at a table, alone, with her head down. Brock went over to her.

"Come on, Abby, it's time to go," Mr. Ferguson began.

"I want to stay for a little bit longer. If you want to go back, then it's fine by me, but I don't feel like it right now," Abigail said.

"We came here together and have to leave together. We can't miss our bus. Now let's go. I don't want to get caught in the rain," Brock replied.

"I said that I want to stay for a little bit longer. Now leave me be," Abigail added.

"It seems like you're drunk," Mr. Ferguson told her.

"What if I am?" asked Abigail. "You need to go home and lay down to sleep it off. Now, I'm only going to say it one more time: it's time to leave. Either you come, or I will make you," Brock answered.

Abigail then got up and walked with the others to the bus stop, leaving only Albert Swindle and Spyder behind.

"I hope we didn't make a mistake by joining forces with those bums. From the stories I've heard about them, they can be very unpredictable at times. We better use as much caution as we can," Mr. Swindle began.

"Do you think you're any better?" inquired Spyder.

"I may be a traveling man, but compared to them, I have it much better. I'm going to be on my way now because I have a long drive ahead of me. I need to get on the road before the rain comes down again. I will contact you soon with an update," Albert Swindle said as he got up and left the pub to return to his caravan.

Spyder sat there alone for a moment before standing up to leave the pub. On his way out, he stopped to talk to the man who was playing guitar and singing.

"I'll pay you a dollar to stop making all of that awful noise. Then maybe you can use it to get some music lessons for yourself," Spyder told him, pulling out a one-dollar bill and handing it to him.

The man said nothing but looked as though he had just had his heart ripped out. Spyder then left the pub.

Everything was falling into place for them now that they had developed another conspiracy. Initially, it was a plot for revenge that Albert Swindle put together, but it had expanded since then. Now that the homeless people had joined the fray, there was an even better chance of them getting away with kidnapping Trevor.

They knew that breaking into the house wasn't an option and completely ruled that out. They had to devise a way to somehow lure Trevor out of the house. That wasn't going to be easy, but with the creativeness of Mr. Swindle and the cleverness of Spyder combined, they would hatch an ideal way to make it happen. However they did it, one thing was for sure: they would be relentless until they got what they were pursuing.

CHAPTER 5

Contains Fresh Discoveries of Trevor's Family Tree and Something Incredible Is Revealed

Ever since he started his research about Trevor's family history, Norman devoted many hours to uncovering all the information that could be found about and traced back to finally discovering Trevor's true identity. So far, a lot had been revealed, which no one, not even Norman himself, could believe. He still wanted to know if Trevor was his sister's child, and it became an obsession to the point where Norman stayed in his office night and day, only going out to eat meals. Then he would go right back into his office again. This made his nieces very concerned about his well-being, so much so that both Margaret and Rhonda were barely able to sleep and lay awake for a few hours before finally falling asleep.

On another rainy morning, Margaret and Birdie sat at the table in the kitchen, drinking a freshly brewed and hot cup of coffee as they watched the rain fall down through the window. They couldn't help but feel concerned again. "What do you think Uncle Norman is doing in his office?" asked Rhonda.

"I wish I knew. He's been acting so strange these last few weeks, and it wasn't like this before. If only he could tell us, then we might understand why he's so determined about something, and I wonder what it is," Margaret answered.

"Is Trevor still asleep?" inquired Birdie.

"No, he got up a few hours ago before I did and is in the living room. I already checked on him a few minutes ago," Margaret replied.

"I just hope that we find out why Uncle Norman hasn't been himself. I'm very worried about him, to be quite honest," Rhonda began, taking the last sip of her coffee and then letting out a sigh.

"Do you want some more coffee?" asked Margaret.

"Maybe I will have just a little bit. It will help calm my nerves about this whole thing with Uncle Norman," Birdie answered.

Just then, to their surprise, Norman walked into the room. He looked very conflicted about something. "Are you two busy right now?" inquired Norman.

"No, we're just sitting having some coffee and watching the rain," Rhonda replied.

"That's good because I need to speak with both of you in my office right now. There's something that I have to tell you," Norman told them. Margaret and Birdie got up and followed their uncle into his office. When they got there, they all sat down.

"What is the meaning of this, Uncle?" asked Margaret.

"You aren't going to believe this, but you must because I found proof that my assumption had been right. Not even I was prepared for news like this," Norman replied. "What are you talking about?" inquired Rhonda. "Remember that portrait of my sister that is in the attic? Well, I did some more research, dug a little deeper, and it was confirmed that Trevor is, in fact, my grandson and your first cousin," Norman answered.

Both women looked shocked and appalled at what they had just heard and looked as though they had seen a ghost. "How is that possible, Uncle?" inquired Margaret.

"I found more information on Trevor's family tree, and sure enough, I was on there, and so was my sister, as well as the two of you. I know this is big news and might be hard to process, but I have the paper right here," Norman replied, holding up a piece of paper with a family tree on it.

"I don't know if I'm ready for something like this. We took Trevor in out of the kindness of our hearts, only to find out now that he's a part of our family. I'm speechless," Birdie added. "We mustn't tell Trevor yet. There will come a time to do it, and now is not that time. We should go about our daily routines as we always do and not give Trevor any reason to think that something is wrong," Norman told them.

"I get it now. That's what you've been doing this whole time, and now it all makes sense. We were so worried about you, but now that we know why you have been in here working, it makes us feel a whole lot better," Margaret began. "Let's adjourn for now. We can talk some more about this later, if you like, after Trevor goes to sleep," Norman said.

It was then that both Margaret and Rhonda got up and went out of the office, still thinking about what their uncle had told them.

"I'm going to go check on Trevor because it's already been a half an hour since the last time that we checked on him, and you did it the last time, so now it's my turn," Birdie began. "While you're doing that, I'm going to make some pancakes for us because I'm craving them and think that something sweet and tasty would be a perfect start to our day since we haven't eaten breakfast yet. Let me do the cooking," Margaret said.

They then went their separate ways. When Rhonda got to the living room, she was surprised to see Trevor lying on the floor, coloring in his coloring book. Birdie didn't want to disturb him because he was heavily immersed in his work. It was then that Trevor looked up from his coloring book.

"Do you need me for something?" he asked.

"No, I just came by to check up on you and to tell you that Margaret is making pancakes for us," Birdie answered.

"Oh boy, I can't wait. I am actually hungry and could use something to eat. Maybe tomorrow you can make french toast for us. I sure would like to try that," Trevor added.

"Perhaps another time. It should be ready in a few minutes. I will come back and get you when they're done. You can keep coloring until then. It shouldn't be too much longer," Margaret told him.

"Can I have extra syrup on mine?" asked Trevor.

"We only have the sugar-free kind, so you can have as much as you like. I have to do a couple of things but will be back once the pancakes are ready," Margaret replied.

She then left. After a few minutes, the pancakes were finally finished. Luckily for Margaret, she had finished everything she needed to do and came back to get Trevor. When he got to the kitchen table, the others sat down and waited.

"Where's the spatula?" inquired Rhonda.

"It's in the middle drawer. I moved it to make room for something else that wouldn't fit in any of the other ones. I'll go get the syrup and put it on the table," Margaret answered.

Without them knowing, Red Stranger and Doc had infiltrated their backyard and were hiding behind a wall, still able to observe what was happening inside the house. Margaret then sat down at the table after placing the syrup on it. Soon enough, the pancakes were served. Trevor began with one on his plate and then had a second helping of two more, smothering them with extra syrup.

After breakfast, Trevor went back to coloring for a little bit, then he grew tired and went upstairs to his room to put away his coloring stuff. When he went back down, he joined Margaret and Birdie in the living room.

"Are you all finished coloring for the day?" asked Rhonda.

"Yes, I already did three pages and want to save the others for when I feel like doing them," Trevor replied.

"What do you want to do now?" inquired Margaret.

"I have an idea. Let's do an art project. We have a whole box of materials for that. It's in the cabinet near Uncle Norman's office, but there's so much stuff in there it may be hard to find," Birdie answered. "I think I saw it the other day when I was going through looking for something. If I'm right, it should be there. I'll go and get it so we can get started right away," Margaret said as she got up and left to get the box of art supplies.

When she went back, they started on their art project, which involved making pictures out of macaroni. The good thing was that they could make whatever they wanted. Margaret and Rhonda already had an idea and were working diligently at it.

"Am I doing this right?" asked Trevor.

"Yes, just remember you have to glue each piece down carefully where you want it," Birdie replied. Trevor continued to make his picture, but he was just putting stuff on different parts of the paper. While he was working, Trevor looked at the window and saw two things moving very fast away from the house. He couldn't make out what they were because they were gone before he could figure it out.

"What's wrong, Trevor?" inquired Margaret.

"I thought I saw two things moving very fast away from our house. I hope it wasn't those bad people again," Trevor answered, then went back to his art project.

"Do you want me to get our uncle?" asked Rhonda.

"No, that's alright. I'm sure that it wasn't them. I might just be seeing things that aren't there," Trevor replied.

Every now and then, Trevor kept looking out the window, but the two blurs that he saw weren't there. They were actually Red Stranger and

Doc, who were now hiding across the street between two houses but then took a shortcut so as not to be seen again.

"Are you almost done?" inquired Trevor.

"Yes, I just have a few more pieces to put on, then it will be finished, and I will let the picture dry," Margaret answered.

"What about you?" Birdie asked Margaret.

"I'm almost done myself. I think it would be good if we hang them up on the refrigerator to display them," Rhonda replied.

Just then, Norman walked into the room. "There you three are, I was wondering what you were up to," he began.

"We were just doing an art project, but we're just about done with it," Margaret said. "I could sure use some help because I made a little mess," Trevor replied. He had glue all over his hands, and some was on the paper, as well.

"Let's get you cleaned up, then I will do the rest for you. But Margaret and I have to make lunch before that," Birdie added. It was at that point when she and Trevor left the living room and went into the kitchen to wash all the glue off Trevor's hands. Once that was done, Margaret and Rhonda started making lunch for them.

When it was ready, they ate, then Birdie finished Trevor's picture, and they put all three pictures on the refrigerator, which made it more artsy because before there was nothing on the refrigerator. Even though Norman knew the truth about his sister having a child and that child happened to be Trevor, he was still, nonetheless, very perplexed about how the whole thing had come about without him even knowing. This carried over for the remainder of the day, and while they were eating dinner, it showed even more.

"Is there something wrong, Uncle?" inquired Margaret.

"No, I just have some stuff on my mind, that's all. But I'm fine otherwise," Norman answered.

"It doesn't seem that way. Whenever there's something wrong, Margaret and I can tell right away, and you know that you can't hide something like that from us," Rhonda added.

"Why do you think that?" asked Norman.

"I think I know what it is, and let's talk about it later after Trevor goes to sleep. That would be the right time for us to do it," Margaret replied.

After dinner, Trevor stayed up for a little while longer. Then, when he started to get tired, he went upstairs to sleep. That gave Norman and his two nieces the perfect opportunity to talk. They sat in the living room together. Margaret drank a glass of white wine while they were conversing.

"You are going to tell us what's wrong?" inquired Birdie.

"I did some more research on our family history and found out that we have a lot more family members than we thought," Norman answered. "What else did you find out?" asked Margaret.

"The man who my sister married, his name was Ronald Donner. He was the youngest of four children and was born out of wedlock. He quit school at a young age and joined the army and served in the Vietnam War," Norman told them.

"How did you find all of this out?" asked Margaret.

"I found some old family documents in the attic when Trevor and I were in there. At the time, I didn't think that they were accurate, but after seeing the portrait of my sister and the resemblance of her in Trevor, I knew that it had to be true," Norman replied.

"I don't even know that we had an Uncle Ronald because our mother never spoke about him. There must be a good reason for that," Rhonda began. "You were actually named after him, and he was both of your godfathers. I didn't approve of such a thing, but your parents insisted, so I couldn't argue with them," Norman said.

"Where were these documents that you found?" inquired Birdie.

"They were scattered on an old chair. I only saw a little bit of what it said; there was more than one paper. I'm thinking about going back up there and retrieving them so I can further understand this whole situation more clearly," Norman answered.

"This is all so fascinating that I don't know what to think about it. Who would have thought that the boy that showed up on our doorstep and has been living with us ever since is one of our relatives? But in a way, it makes me happy because before we knew this, Trevor was already kind of part of our family," Margaret added.

Norman noticed that Margaret was almost done with her wine. "Are you going to have another glass?" he asked.

"No, I think that I'll only have one so not to overdo it. That's happened to me before, and every time, I always regretted it," Margaret replied.

"Did you see anything else on those documents?" inquired Rhonda.

"Yes, there was a lot more written on them, but because I was with Trevor, I didn't want to take them yet," Norman answered.

"When do you plan to go back up there to get them?" asked Margaret.

"I have to do it when Trevor is asleep so that he won't ask me about the papers. I was thinking maybe tomorrow night I would venture up there since it's already late now," Norman replied.

"We would like to know, as well, what's on those documents. It could also really help with your research and for us to find out more about our family," Birdie told them.

"I'm still trying to figure out who is supposed to be on that blank spot on our family tree and why they don't appear. There has to be a good explanation behind it," Norman began. "Well, whoever it is, they must not want anything to do with our family. Otherwise, they wouldn't have left a blank spot where they're supposed to be on the tree," Margaret said.

"Would you look at the time? It's almost eleven o'clock. We really should be off to bed and can talk about this some more tomorrow night after Trevor goes to sleep," Norman replied.

They all stood up and left the living room to go upstairs to bed. Margaret didn't even bother to take her glass, which she had been drinking from, to the kitchen. She left it on the coffee table.

Once everyone was asleep, it was quiet throughout the house, as it always is at that hour. However, Rhonda awoke suddenly and heard footsteps walking down the hallway. Her first thought was that the bad people had returned and broken into the house, intending to harm Trevor. It made a lot of sense because Trevor had earlier told Margaret and Birdie that he had seen two things moving very fast; perhaps it was them.

Then, Rhonda remembered the documents that were in the attic and thought it might just be Norman going up to get them. She didn't know what to do; if it was the bad people, they might hurt her if she tried to be brave and stand up to them. Birdie was frozen in fear; she could feel her heart beating very fast. But she couldn't just lie there and let them hurt Trevor. She got out of bed and walked over to the door, opening it very fast. Sure enough, it was only Norman; he had gone up to the attic to get the documents. Rhonda then shut her door, got back into bed, and fell back to sleep.

They all wondered what else was written on those documents. Tomorrow night, more would be revealed to them. The whole thing was quite complicated at the present moment, and they hoped to gain some clarity that would help them discover not only their entire family history but also Trevor's true identity.

CHAPTER 6

Two Old Enemies of Trevor Run Away to Miami and Get a Tempting Offer from a Familiar Character

Sometime after midnight, while everyone was warm and cozy in their beds, dreaming of faraway fantasy worlds that surpassed the mundane reality people often loathe and wish to escape from, two figures ventured forth. The night, with its eerie ambiance, cast shadows as streetlights burned brightly like beacons of hope amid the darkness. Daylight loomed closer, gradually replacing the night's veil, marking the passage of time as minutes slipped away.

In the dead of night, Ezra Cooper and Zoey walked along the highway. They carried only what they needed, having left their foster home around ten o'clock, embarking on their journey to Miami. "Can we stop to rest for a second?" asked Zoey. "We don't have time for that," replied Ezra. "We have to keep going if we plan to make it to Miami before daylight."

"I'm tired and thirsty," Zoey complained. "I don't think I can go any further without resting or having a drink."

"Stop your complaining," Ezra retorted. "There should be a city up ahead where we can get something to eat and drink. But for now, let's keep going." They pressed on.

"We have to budget our money because we don't have a lot to spend on things," Zoey reminded him.

"Don't worry about that," Ezra reassured her. "We will manage. Besides, you did steal some money from the Evanses before we left, so if we need to, we can somehow get more."

"I stole it for you, Ezra dear, so we had some extra cash for our journey," Zoey explained. "It made it easier because I knew where they hid their valuables and money."

"Look, it's only three more miles until we reach Fort Lauderdale," Ezra observed, reading a sign on the side of the road. "I think that would be the best place to rest and get something to eat. I haven't eaten in hours and am starving."

"I think I can hold out until then," Zoey replied. "It's not much further anyway, and as long as I'm with you, then I know that I can make it." They continued to walk.

When they finally made it to Fort Lauderdale, both Ezra and Zoey looked for a place to rest and eat. There were so many different restaurants and bars in the area of Oakland Park they didn't know which one to choose.

"This place sounds good to me, the Old Sea Captain," Ezra told her, reading a neon sign that was across the street from where they were.

"The old what?" asked Zoey.

"Sea Captain. It appears to be a pub. Let's go check it out," Ezra replied, and they hurried across the street and went into the Old Sea Captain pub.

Once the two were inside, there weren't many people, and the jukebox was on, playing music. Both Ezra and Zoey looked and saw that there were a lot of empty tables available for them to sit at.

"I think that one over there by the window is a good place to sit," Ezra told her, pointing to a table in the back of the pub.

They then went over to it and sat down.

"Can I get something to drink?" asked Zoey.

"Sure, whatever you like. This is the start of our new life. No more living in someone else's house under their room and rules. We're free to do whatever we like. I can become a well-respected gentleman, and if you like, you can be a lady," Ezra answered.

Not too far away from them at the bar was Albert Swindle. He had been traveling around for days and had returned to the place where he had first met Spyder and had forged a relationship with the homeless people, as well. Mr. Swindle sat there drinking while also listening to Ezra and Zoey's conversation. He was intrigued by what they were saying.

"Do you want another drink?" inquired Zeke.

"Yes, but this time, get me something different, like some tequila. I could use a stronger drink right about now," Albert Swindle replied.

"Hush, my friend. It looks as though we have some new blood from the north. What an interesting pair they are," the African American bartender added.

"What's their story?" asked Albert Swindle.

"I don't know. You were the one who was eavesdropping on them, so you tell me. Children aren't allowed in here anyway," Zeke answered.

"I am going to go talk to them and find out," Mr. Swindle began, and he got up and walked over to the back where Ezra and Zoey were. They were still in the middle of talking.

"You don't think the police will find us and make us go back?" inquired Zoey.

"No, of course not. They could send a whole search party after us, but they still wouldn't be able to find us. We're in the clearing," Ezra answered.

They then saw Albert Swindle standing before them.

"What do you want, sir?" asked Ezra.

"I couldn't help but overhear you two talking and understand your situation very well. Therefore, I have a proposal for you both to come work for me," Mr. Swindle replied.

"We would like to, but first, we need to get to know each other before making any kind of agreements," Ezra said.

"What are your names?" inquired Albert Swindle.

"I am Robert Porter, and this is Mrs. Porter. We're looking for employment that will benefit us both. If you are serious about this, then we need to know more," Robert Porter replied.

"I can tell that you have come a long way from where you first began. It shows more than you think," Mr. Swindle added.

"How do you know that?" asked Robert Porter.

"Because we don't have that dirt around here," Albert Swindle answered, pointing down to the mud that was all over both of the two children's shoes.

"What's the pay like?" inquired Robert Porter.

"You will live comfortably, get paid on a weekly basis, and have all of the food and drinks that you want," Mr. Swindle replied.

"That sounds very promising, and I think that my wife agrees," Robert Porter said. "Yes, Ezra—I mean, Robert, dear, it does," Zoey began.

It was then that Albert Swindle put his finger to his nose, and Robert Porter imitated it. "I will say that you have a very sharp mind, Mr. Porter, and I can tell that you will make me proud," Mr. Swindle said.

"I don't like to brag, but when I put my mind to something, I can definitely get stuff done—that I can say with all honesty," Robert

Porter replied. "I need to get some more spray before I leave here because I only have a little bit left in the can that I have now," Albert Swindle added.

"What do you need that for?" asked Robert Porter.

"It keeps the cockroaches away when I'm sleeping. They tend to show up more in the summer months than any other time," Mr. Swindle replied.

"Do you live in the woods or something?" inquired Robert Porter.

"Not exactly. I live off the grid and do a lot of traveling from one place to another. It's part of my business," Albert Swindle answered. "Can you get me another drink, Robert, dear?" asked Mrs. Porter.

"Allow me, and don't worry about having to pay because whatever drinks you want are all on me," Mr. Swindle replied.

"What kind of business are you in?" asked Robert Porter.

"I'm glad you asked. I happen to be a magician, and one who is world-famous and has been for before you were even born. I'm currently looking for an assistant who can help me with my shows," Mr. Swindle answered.

"I would volunteer, but the truth is I don't know anything about magic or how to do it," Robert Porter told him.

"Would you like to learn?" inquired Mr. Swindle.

"Yes, if you can teach me, then I would be grateful and would practice as much as possible to be able to get all the stuff correct," Robert Porter replied.

"I would be glad to, but you have to earn your keep first before I can make you my assistant. I don't just let anyone do that without having to work for me in the beginning, but I can also employ your wife, as well, so that the two of you are together," Mr. Swindle began.

"What would we have to do?" asked Mrs. Porter.

"Just a few simple things that don't take a long time to do. I can start you right away since you're both so eager to work. I have some room in my place for two more people," Albert Swindle answered.

"What do you live?" asked Robert Porter.

"I could tell you, but I'd rather show you instead. It's a little cramped on the inside, but I still don't mind calling it my home," Mr. Swindle replied.

"Do you live in a mobile home?" inquired Mrs. Porter.

"Something like that. I prefer it over having a house or apartment where there are other people around. I like to have peace and quiet all the time," Albert Swindle answered.

"As much as we'd like to come and work for you, we want to have multiple options about where we live and work. We'll have to get back to you when we make our decisions. It was nice meeting you," Mr. Robert Porter said.

"I'm Albert Swindle. I apologize for not giving my name to you when we first met. It's just that I have to keep a low profile for my own reasons. It's nothing personal," Mr. Swindle replied.

They were just about to leave before Mr. Swindle panicked and stood up. 'Wait, don't go yet. I need your answer soon. Otherwise, I will search for other people. Either you say yes or no,'" Albert Swindle added.

"How much do you plan to pay us?" asked Robert Porter.

"I usually start everyone out with ten dollars an hour, but I do it just as a trial basis to see how you will do. If you do well, then I will consider raising your pay and possibly appointing you to be my assistant. But you have to prove yourself to me," Mr. Swindle replied.

"We'll do whatever we have to if it's for money, because we only have a little bit that we took with us before we left where we were before," Robert Porter added.

"Do you live alone?" inquired Mrs. Porter.

"No, I have a boy who is already employed with me but has no desire to learn magic, so I just let him work and live with me," Albert Swindle answered.

"Where are we to sleep?" asked Robert Porter.

"I have an extra bedroom that has only one bed and an air mattress, but if you prefer it, I also have a couch in the living room. It's not that big, but it's very comfortable," Mr. Swindle replied.

"Well, it would be better than sleeping outside, so being without work or enough money to live, and since we just got here, we'll take you up on your offer, just as long as you keep your end of the bargain," Robert Porter told him.

"Do you want to know a secret?" inquired Albert Swindle.

"Yes, please do tell us," Mrs. Porter answered.

"Never cut corners when it comes to working, and always do an accurate job, and you'll never have to worry about struggling ever again. That's something I don't tell everyone," Mr. Swindle began.

"Is that how you made your money?" asked Robert Porter.

"Yes, it's how I started, but with time, I climbed the ladder up to the top. That takes time, but if you stick with me, I can get you there," Albert Swindle replied.

"We're really supposed to be on our way to Miami. That's where the two of us planned to go. We only stopped here to rest for a little bit," Robert Porter said.

"I can take you there. I have to go there to meet some people and will take you the rest of the way so that you don't have to walk," Mr. Swindle replied.

"We would really appreciate that because we have come such a long way and are very tired from our travels. That would certainly make it easier for us," Robert Porter began.

"How do we know that you're legit?" inquired Mrs. Porter. "I can do a magic trick for you as proof, and I know the perfect one. If one of you has a quarter that I can use, then give it to me," Albert Swindle answered.

Both Robert Porter and Mrs. Porter checked their pockets but couldn't find a quarter. "We don't have any. All we have is dollar bills on us," Robert Porter replied. "That's alright, I just happen to have one here," Mr. Swindle added as he pulled a small purple pouch from his pocket, took out a quarter, then put the pouch back.

"What are you going to do with that?" asked Robert Porter.

"You will soon see. Notice that I have the quarter in my hand." Swindle then closed his hand, tapped on his knuckle, and reopened it, but the quarter was gone.

"How did you do that?" inquired Mrs. Porter.

"Wait, the trick isn't over yet. There are still two more steps left," Mr. Swindle replied. He then closed his other hand, tapped on his knuckle again, and reopened it, and the quarter was now there and in his other hand. "What do you think now?" inquired Albert Swindle.

"Well, that was very impressive, and no one who wasn't a magician could do something like that, which proves to us your authenticity. But I never doubted you for a minute. It was her that was skeptical," Robert Porter answered. "I just wanted to make sure that you really were who you said you are and not actually a fraud trying to lead us astray. There are a lot of phony people in this world who pass themselves off as real but aren't," Mrs. Porter said. "It's all good; I don't blame you for being cautious, but I have never steered anyone who worked for me wrong. I have too much dignity to do something like that," Mr. Swindle replied.

"Can you teach me that trick?" asked Robert Porter. "Yes, but once you get more advanced in your training, there are some easier ones that I teach first just so people can get a feel for how magic really works with different magicians. There are different variations of tricks," Albert Swindle replied.

"I understand that, but I'm open to learning whatever you teach me, no matter the difficulty level or how it's taught," Robert Porter added.

"Well, you certainly have the right attitude and determination, which I admire greatly. I have no doubt that you will be a great asset to my business, Mr. Porter. I hope that your wife is just the same," Mr. Swindle told him.

"What do you mean by that?" inquired Mrs. Porter.

"Only that I can tell that your husband is ready to work, but you haven't really given me any indication of that whatsoever," Albert Swindle answered.

"Why do you say that?" asked Robert Porter.

"It's not such a big deal. I just want to see if she has the same work ethic as you do. If so, then both of you will make me proud," Mr. Swindle replied.

"When do you want us to begin working?" inquired Robert Porter.

"If you're still not too tired from your journey, then today would be fine because I have to let the other child, that I mentioned before, teach you what you do. He'll make a great mentor to the two of you, of that, I am sure. We should be on our way now. Follow me, and I will show you where it is that I live," Mr. Swindle answered.

It was then that all three of them got up and went out of the pub and into the parking lot where Albert Swindle's caravan was parked. At first, Robert Porter and Mrs. Porter didn't really know what to think about such a confined living space, but they knew that having a roof over their heads again was satisfying compared to having to sleep out in the open. Both of them made the best of their new home. Robert Porter slept on the bed while Mrs. Porter took the air mattress until Mr. Swindle woke them up a few hours later to tell them to start working. The only thing that they didn't care for in the caravan was the stuffed heads, which creeped them out; however, they tried their best to tolerate it as best they could.

Even though it was much different from living in a foster home and was a big transition, Robert Porter and Mrs. Porter adjusted well to their new lives like a duck to water. They planned to remain in Fort Lauderdale for a few more hours before getting on the road to Miami. Fate had stepped in, and Robert Porter and Mrs. Porter were finally living the dream lives.

CHAPTER 7

Describes How Ezra Cooper and Zoey Were Employed by Mr. Albert Swindle

So it was that Mr. Ezra Cooper, otherwise known as Robert Porter, and Zoey had officially been employed by Albert Swindle. They had never dreamed that after leaving their foster home and running away, things would turn in their favor so quickly. Had they not stopped to rest where they did and met Mr. Swindle, it would have become a struggle for survival. Luckily for them, they had acquired a place to live and employment at the same time, although it wasn't the kind of life they were accustomed to. They were fulfilling their needs, unlike where they had come from, and were slowly but surely adapting to their new living situation.

Robert Porter and Mrs. Porter got a few hours of sleep before they had to go to work, but it wasn't enough. While they were eating their breakfast along with Nathan, whom they had just met not too long ago, Robert Porter began, "I think this is the kind of life I could grow to like a lot, even if it's not the most luxurious."

"Only think for yourself, my boy. That really helps a lot without clouding your judgment and causing you not to be able to think clearly," Mr. Swindle said.

"Ha, that's what you think. I can't be persuaded to do things based on promises or ultimatums. I negotiate things so that it's mutual between myself and the other person," Robert Porter replied with a laugh.

"Is there any more toast?" asked Mrs. Porter.

"I don't give seconds on food. Whatever you get, you eat and like it because I can't afford a lot to feed the three of you and myself. Now, get to work, all of you," Albert Swindle answered after they had finished eating. Robert Porter, Mrs. Porter, and Nathan went out of the caravan and started on their work, which was to clean the outside of the entire caravan.

Nathan mentored both Robert Porter and Mrs. Porter at the same time, showing them how to do it. The morning sun made them hot and tired, but they still worked.

"When are we going to go to Miami?" inquired Robert Porter.

"Whenever Swindle decides it's time, he'll let us know. Until then, we have to work because if he comes out here and sees that we're goofing off, he'll get very angry. And I haven't told you what it's like when that happens," Nathan replied.

"He doesn't scare me. I'm not afraid of anyone or anything. He wouldn't dare lay one hand on me because I would just fight back without even hesitating to knock him out, even if it cost me my life. But that would prove to him and you just how tough I really am," Robert Porter added.

"Why don't you try it then?" inquired Nathan. "Maybe I should start with you first as a warm-up. I predict that you'll be on the ground in less than two seconds from when we begin."

Just then, Albert Swindle went out of the caravan. He was smoking a cigar and humming loudly.

"Why aren't you working?" he asked.

"We are, but we're taking our time and are already halfway done. We just need to do the top of the caravan," Nathan replied.

"You three better finish up because I have more for you to do inside and need it done before the day is over," Mr. Swindle told them.

"When did you start smoking cigars?" inquired Nathan.

"I always have, but I only do it when I'm in the mood. I have more where this came from in boxes stashed away where only I know where they are," Albert Swindle answered.

"You can't force me to go up there. I don't like being up high, so one of you will just have to do it," Robert Porter added.

"Do you expect me to?" asked Mrs. Porter.

"Well, someone has to, and it's not going to be me unless he wants to when we're both off the hook. But like I said, I wouldn't be caught dead up there where it's easy to fall," Robert Porter replied, pointing to Nathan.

"I don't care who does it. It has to be done now. Hurry up, you only have a few hours left to finish everything before we leave," Mr. Swindle began, and then he went back inside the caravan.

"If you two aren't going to go up and clean the top of the caravan, then it looks like I have to pick up the slack," Nathan said.

"Is he saying that we're going to Miami?" inquired Robert Porter.

"Yes, but only because he has to meet with some people about something important that he's doing with them," Nathan answered. He went behind the caravan to get the ladder and climbed up to clean the top while Robert Porter and Mrs. Porter just stood there watching him work.

From inside the caravan, Albert Swindle saw this and was furious with his new recruits. He was sitting on the couch in the living room and could see and hear everything because he was by the window, watching their every move. "Why are you standing around?" he asked. Both Robert Porter and Mrs. Porter jumped in surprise and quickly went back to working. They could hear Mr. Swindle mumbling to himself while he smoked his cigar. The smell was nauseating, but they knew they had no choice but to put up with it.

Once Nathan was done cleaning the top of the caravan, he waited for their next instructions. Shortly after, Albert Swindle went out of the caravan again, still smoking the same cigar. He looked at the caravan then turned to his pupils. "You three did well. Now, I need you to come inside because there's some more work to be done," he told them.

They followed him inside the caravan, and once there, he handed them rags and bottles of cleaning liquid. "What do we need these for?" Robert Porter asked.

"I'm glad you asked, Mr. Porter. The three of you wipe down all of my knickknacks that are in here and inside my room, as well. Now, get working! Time is money, you know," Mr. Swindle replied, and then he went back to sitting on the couch.

"You two can do in here while I do the ones in Swindle's room," Nathan added.

"Who died and made you the boss?" inquired Mrs. Porter.

"Well, I've been here longer than both of you and was put in charge of you by Swindle, so you have to listen to what I say," Nathan answered.

"That may be true, but it's a team effort if we want to get all of this stuff done, and none of us should be above another because it only causes friction between us," Robert Porter began.

Mr. Swindle gave him a piercing look, signaling not to be defiant and to do whatever he was told.

"Do you think that you should decide?" asked Nathan.

"Maybe I do, and if you allow me to, I will make you do this room while Mrs. Porter and myself do the other. And if you don't like it, that's too bad," Robert Porter replied.

"Enough of this bickering already! I shall decide who does what room since the three of you can't do it. Mr. Porter and Mrs. Porter will be in this room while Nathan does my room. Get to work! We only have a few hours left before we have to be on the road," Albert Swindle replied.

"There are so many of them. It might take us forever to do them. I think I'll rest for a little bit on the couch with you while Mrs. Porter gets a head start, then I will join in," Robert Porter added.

"Do you want to be confined to your room for a week?" inquired Mr. Swindle.

"You wouldn't dare do that. These two aren't capable of doing the work without me. I am what guides them along," Robert Porter answered.

"Don't tempt me, Mr. Porter. If you continue to act up, then I will do it. And if you happen to try and sneak out, I will punish you even more until you learn to follow orders," Albert Swindle told him.

"Alright, then I'll listen, and Mrs. Porter and I will wipe in here. But we should really alternate. That way, it's fair," Robert Porter began.

"Life isn't fair, Mr. Porter. That's a fact of life. Someday you will realize that. Now all three of you need to get to work," Mr. Swindle said. At that moment, they started wiping down all the knickknacks that were in both rooms.

Later on, when they were all finished with their work, Albert Swindle allowed them to rest in their room. All of a sudden, they could feel the caravan moving. Robert Porter looked out the small window of their room and could see things passing by very fast. He knew that they were now on their way down to Miami. It didn't take them that long to get there. When they did, they drove to the liquor store where the homeless people always hung out. Mr. Swindle told Robert, Nathan, and Mrs. Porter to wait for him while he got a drink for himself. They went behind the store where Brock Ferguson, Red Stranger, Doc, and Abigail were all standing around in their usual spot, talking.

"I had a feeling that you were coming after not hearing from me in a while, but I've been very busy with other things and haven't found the time to contact you or Spyder," Mr. Ferguson began. "I figured that and thought, why not take a trip down to come see you? After all, I wasn't too far from here," Albert Swindle said.

"Who are they?" asked Red Stranger.

"They are my employees, Nathan, who had been with me a long time," Swindle replied. "And these two are new and fresh from the north."

"Do they have names?" inquired Doc.

"Yes, this is Mr. Robert Porter and his wife, Mrs. Porter. We met just a day ago. Only began working for me today," Albert Swindle replied.

"They feel awfully young to be married, and I'm older than they are," Abigail told him.

"My dear girl, people can marry at whatever age they want nowadays. I myself was surprised when I heard that," Mr. Swindle began.

"Enough of this talking. We need to talk business now. I spoke to Spyder the other day, and he still wants us to wait on kidnapping the boy until he says it's time," Brock said.

"I think we should just do it and inform him once it's already done. It's not going to help us if we take our time doing this," Abigail replied.

"Don't talk foolish, girl. We have to go by what Spyder says. If we were to go on our own, then he would have a fit. That's why we're not doing it that way. When Spyder told me that when he's not around, you all have to take orders from either Mr. Swindle or myself, and none of you will question our authority. Got it?" Mr. Ferguson told them. They all nodded to show that they understood.

"Who is it that you are going to kidnap?" inquired Mrs. Porter.

"A boy by the name of Trevor Conway. He's a horrible child who we all want to get rid of for good, and perhaps you two can help out with that," Albert Swindle answered.

"Isn't that the boy who was in our foster home?" asked Robert Porter.

"Yes, Robert dear. He made our lives miserable, and after he left, we thought that it would get better but it didn't, and that's why we left," Mrs. Porter replied.

"I had no idea that you two knew him. It looks like we all have something in common: that we hate Trevor and want that boy out of our hair forever. With all of us working as one, we can definitely make that a reality," Mr. Swindle began.

"How can we help?" asked Robert Porter.

"You and Mrs. Porter will be our backup just in case something were to go wrong. We already have enough people to do the job, but the two of you will stay here while we get the boy," Brock answered.

It was then that Albert Swindle took a large sip of his drink. "Come now, Mr. Swindle, don't bogart that drink if you can't share it with the rest of us," Abigail said.

"Go get your own. I paid for this with my own money and don't have to share it with anyone if I don't want to," Albert Swindle replied.

"Stop it, you two. Now, once we have the boy, we will come here first to pick up Robert and Mrs. Porter then go straight to Red Stranger's spot to hide out," Mr. Ferguson told them.

"Aren't we going to congregate here?" inquired Doc.

"There's been a slight change of plans. Our new meeting place is going to be this boy's spot. It's better because it's hidden, and no one will see us," Mr. Swindle replied, pointing to Red Stranger.

"Why can't we just come here and stay?" asked Red Stranger.

"Because there are people all around here, and they will get suspicious and possibly call the police. That's why we need somewhere that's hidden away," Brock answered.

"It's not exactly that hidden, you know. Someone can still see what it is that we're doing," Abigail added.

"We already have a plan if that were to happen. We would all act casual until they pass by. They have no reason to suspect anything if they don't see anything out of the ordinary," Mr. Ferguson began.

"Now that we've got everything figured out, soon the boy will belong to us again. Then we can put him out of his misery and get the money. I just love it when a plan comes together," Albert Swindle said, rubbing his hands together.

"Spyder says that he wants us to do the job sometime between the end of this month and the beginning of the next one," Brock replied.

"Then that's when we shall put our plan into action. Until then, we have to be patient. It will be here before we know it," Mr. Swindle added.

"I just hope that there aren't any cops in the area that day. Otherwise, it will make it much more difficult for us to kidnap Trevor," Red Stranger told them.

"What would we do then?" inquired Doc.

"They won't stay for too long if they see that nothing is going on. We'll have to wait it out to be safe, and once they're gone, we can spring into action," Mr. Ferguson replied.

It was then that Abigail started to walk away. "Where are you going at this time of night?" asked Brock.

"I just want to take a walk, that's all. I need to get some exercise because I've been very tired lately, and I think that might help," Abigail answered.

"We haven't finished our discussion yet, so you will not go anywhere until I say you can," Mr. Ferguson began.

"I need to take a walk, and that's the truth. Now, please let me go for my walk. You can always fill me in with what was said later," Abigail said as she again tried to walk away.

"You're not going anywhere. I'll stop you if I have to. When I say stay, you stay," Mr. Ferguson replied.

Just as Abigail attempted to walk away again, she was stopped by Brock, who grabbed her and held her in his arms. Abigail was kicking and screaming, trying to break free. "Let me go! I told you I'm just going for a walk, and that's it!" Abigail shouted.

Mr. Ferguson then walked over to the closet wall and threw her against it. "Now, stay there and don't even think about moving," he told her.

"Why, my dear girl, you look absolutely tan," Albert Swindle added.

"Tan?" cried Abigail, looking at her arms. "It's nothing that I'm doing. I don't go out in the sun all that much," she began.

"Did Mr. Spyder tell you anything else?" inquired Red Stranger.

"No, it was a very short conversation because he had stuff to do. But he said that he will see us soon and to not do anything without his consent first," Brock replied.

"Who is it that you're talking about?" asked Mrs. Porter.

"I'll tell you. He's Trevor's cousin who told us that the boy's parents left a will that has money in it to him. And if we dispose of the boy, we will get the money for ourselves. Of course, Mr. Spyder, Mr. Ferguson, and myself get the most, but there's still a lot of it to go around," Mr. Swindle answered.

"How do you plan to do it?" inquired Robert Porter.

"Spyder will be the one to do it because he came up with the whole thing, and since the boy is his family, it would only be right to let him," Mr. Ferguson replied.

"There is only one more matter that we must settle, and that's how much we plan to give the children for their help. After all, we wouldn't be able to do it without them," Albert Swindle said.

"We'll have to talk about that with Mr. Spyder and see what he says. But for now, we don't need to worry about that. What's important is that we rub out the boy first then figure out the money after it's done," Brock replied.

"Would you look at the time? We better get going now. It was great to see all of you again. We will talk soon," Mr. Swindle told them, and he motioned for Nathan, Robert Porter, and Mrs. Porter to follow him back to the caravan.

Now that Albert Swindle had two new pupils employed by him, he knew that having an extra pair of hands around would be more useful to him than just having only one. That gave him more time to himself. It also meant that Mr. Swindle could rehearse all his magic tricks without being interrupted, on the off chance that someone would call upon him to do a show for them. But with his most recent failure, he knew it might be a very long time before that ever happened again.

Mr. Swindle had heard that his rival, Woodrow Wiggins, had been mysteriously murdered and the police would figure out who did it. Yet to him, that was a good thing because with Wiggins out of the picture, Albert Swindle might have a good chance of getting called upon to do shows. Or at least that was what he hoped. Things might be turning around for Mr. Swindle, but doing shows was the last thing on his mind right now. Whether it happened or not, only time would tell.

CHAPTER 8

Tells How Red Stranger Got Himself into Trouble

Mr. Albert Swindle, the ringleader of his own operation, awoke early the following morning. He had to do a few things before his pupils got up. The first thing that Mr. Swindle did was eat his breakfast of scrambled eggs, toast, and sausage links. After that, he had a cup of coffee and sat down at the kitchen table to reflect on the last few tough months. Somehow, he managed to get through it.

Albert Swindle and his pupils were staying in Miami for a while until they heard from Spyder. Another thing that he pondered about was if they were to succeed in killing Trevor and gaining the money. Mr. Swindle would have to think very hard about what to do with it. He didn't have a bank account and lived off the money that he made from doing shows.

Before Albert Swindle knew it, his pupils had all awoken, and they sat down and waited to be fed their breakfast. "What are we having to eat?" asked Robert Porter. "I made something special for the three of you. Hold on while I go and get it from the freezer," Mr. Swindle answered, and then he went into the kitchen and took something out of the freezer. He handed them three frozen waffles. "Isn't there anything else?" inquired Mrs. Porter. "No, not unless you want to go to the store yourself and buy something with your own money. Then that's all you're getting for now. Eat up because you have to get to work once you've finished your breakfast," Albert Swindle replied. He then went outside to get some fresh air.

"I have no appetite and think I will just get to work now," Robert Porter began, and he got up, threw his frozen waffle away in the garbage, and went outside to start working. "Well, since this isn't what I thought it was going to be, I, too, might as well get to work. Here, you can have my waffle," Mrs. Porter said, handing her frozen waffle to Nathan then going outside, leaving Nathan all alone in the caravan and with two frozen waffles. Not knowing what he should do with them, Nathan bit into one of the waffles, but it was so hard and cold that he ended up tossing both waffles into the garbage and joining the others outside.

The three children worked tirelessly, cleaning the tires of the caravan with just a rag and a bucket of soapy water. "You need to put more elbow grease into it, Mr. Porter. Otherwise, it will take you longer to finish cleaning that tire," Mr. Swindle told him. "I am doing the best I can. Maybe there's an easier way to get this done because no matter what I do, the stuff on these tires doesn't come off as easily as you think they would," Robert Porter added. "You should spend less time complaining and more time working like I am doing. Perhaps if you would, you'd already be finished by now," Nathan began. "Who says I'm complaining?" asked Robert Porter. "Well, that's how it sounds to me and that you want to take the easy way out and throw in the towel," Nathan answered. "I never said anything of the sort, and if you think I would do that, then you're wrong for even insinuating it," Robert Porter said.

"That's enough, boys. We don't have time for any arguing when there's still a lot more work to be done before we have to leave," Albert Swindle replied. "Where are we going?" asked Nathan. "To meet those people who we met with last night. I have to follow up with Mr. Ferguson and his associates. That is very important. That's all I can tell you. When you're all finished cleaning every tire, I need two people to polish my collection of stuffed heads. I have given it some thought and have decided that the two to do the job are Mr. Porter and Mrs. Porter. If you would follow me into the caravan, I will show you what you have to do," Mr. Swindle answered.

"Yeah, get into the caravan, you two," Nathan told them. "You're really asking for it, and better watch your back," Robert Porter began, and then he and Mrs. Porter followed Albert Swindle into the caravan.

When the day grew shorter and once all the chores had been done, it was time for Mr. Swindle and his pupils to go down to meet the homeless people at the back of the liquor store. When they arrived, the only person who was there was Brock Ferguson and Abigail, along with Mr. Ferguson's dog, Brutus, who was lying down beside him and let out a loud growl upon seeing Albert Swindle, who jumped back a foot in total fear.

"Don't you know the devil when you see him?" asked Brock to his dog. "It seems that your pet has a strong dislike for me and is finally showing it," Mr. Swindle replied.

"I wouldn't say that. He's somewhat of a high-strung dog who is naturally tough, and that's what I like about him," Brock replied.

"Now, Mr. Ferguson, I have come up with a solution to our little dilemma of how we plan to pay the children. I thought of it a few days ago," Albert Swindle told him.

"Don't you 'Mr. Ferguson' me, you low-down, stingy, vile old coot. You know my name, now I want to hear you say it," Brock added.

"Yes, I'm sorry, Brock. It's just—I don't want to be disrespectful to someone like you, who is a hardworking and well-respected person such as yourself. I meant no offense," Mr. Swindle told him.

Just then, Doc came running up to them, out of breath. "I have terrible news. They got him, Mr. Ferguson," he began.

"Who are you talking about?" inquired Albert Swindle.

"Stranger. The police caught him while he was at the median, flying his sign. He tried to talk his way out of it, but it didn't work, and now he's in the slammer, awaiting trial," Doc answered.

They were certainly in a bind to think of Frederick Gillespie being caught flying a sign. They could only imagine what it was like for the imprisoned Stranger.

"That's too bad. He was a hard worker and always careful not to get caught or rat any of us out. But someone has to go to the courtroom for the trial to see what is going to happen," Mr. Ferguson said.

"Send the new people. They don't have any experience and need to get their foot in the door sometime—that is, if they can put in the effort to do so," Doc replied.

"No, it's not our responsibility, and don't talk to me that way. It would be wise not to pick fights with those who are older and stronger than you, little boy," Robert Porter added. "Now let's not fight. We're all friends here. I think that it's best that I decide who it is that goes. Let me think it over for a minute first," Mr. Swindle told them.

"If you really want me to be the one who goes, then at least pay me to do it, because if not, then you can forget even considering me," Robert Porter began.

"It's up to Mr. Swindle, but I will go if I must," Doc said. "Not for anything in the world, my boy. This is not the time to be reckless and let our emotions cloud our judgment. Everything has to be carefully organized," Albert Swindle replied.

"I don't care if I get caught by the police too. Stranger is my buddy, and therefore, I should be the one who attends the trial. And if I know him the way that I do, Stranger will make them all look like fools because he is clever enough to persuade them to see things his way. I can't believe this is happening. Poor Stranger," Doc added as he started to cry.

"Don't you shed a tear for him because he'll be back on the streets in a few days, making even more money than before," Mr. Swindle told him. "I don't think so. If the court finds him guilty, then he will be relocated to the West Coast, where he'll be locked up for a very long time. It's his own fault for not being careful out there, so now he is going to have to deal with his mistake the hard way," Brock began.

"What time is the trial?" asked Abigail.

"It starts at five thirty, which is only one hour from now, so a decision has to be made very soon," Doc replied.

"I've got the answer to our problem. Both Doc and Mr. Porter will go together and report what the outcome was to us after it's all over. Since I'm a generous person, I'll pay both of you for it," Albert Swindle said.

"Won't someone recognize us?" inquired Robert Porter.

"That's why you will go in disguise. I already have something that you can wear in the caravan that belongs to me. It might be a little big on you, but it will be just the thing to keep your identity a secret," Mr. Swindle answered.

At five o'clock, both Doc and Robert Porter went down to the local courthouse and sat with the other people, waiting for the trial to begin.

"All rise for the Honorable Judge Davidson," the bailiff said, and everyone stood up as Judge Davidson entered. He then sat down at his desk. "Bring in the next case," he ordered, and the bailiff went into a back room and escorted Red Stranger, who went in putting up a fight.

"What are the charges?" asked Judge Davidson.

"Panhandling, Your Honor," the bailiff replied.

"Has he been here before?" inquired Judge Davidson.

"No, but he should have a long time ago. It seems this isn't his first offense," the bailiff answered.

"You must already know why you're here and what it is that brought you here," Judge Davidson began.

"Yes, but seeing how I'm forced to be in this place against my will, I deserve to be heard," Red Stranger said.

"You'll get your chance to talk and salt with it, but seeing how you managed to weasel your way out of the last offenses, I won't show you any remorse. So be prepared to face the consequences of committing a crime," Judge Davidson replied.

"This is no dictatorship. I'm an American. I have rights, you know, and should be allowed to exercise them," Red Stranger added.

"In this courtroom, I call the shots, and what I say goes. You will not tell me how to do things," Judge Davidson told him.

It was then that the bailiff handed him a piece of paper. "I hope you know that you're wasting valuable time and mine, as well. I don't have all day to be here," Red Stranger began.

"It says here that your name is Frederick Gillespie and that you have several charges against you already for trespassing. I'm shocked that the police didn't bring you in for those," Judge Davidson said.

"First of all, that is my real name, but I prefer not to go by it. And second of all, I don't remember ever getting any violations for trespassing. You must have me confused with someone else," Red Stranger replied.

"That's not possible. The police know who you are, and apparently, you tried to use a bunch of fake aliases to try and fool them, which didn't work, by the way. But now that won't save you this time," Judge Davidson told him.

"If you must know, my lawyer is having dinner with the president himself. But since he's away and cannot speak for me, I must do it myself," Red Stranger added.

"Where are the witnesses?" inquired Judge Davidson.

"They refused to give us their names, and we don't have any because of that. And I don't think anyone else saw him," the bailiff replied.

"Where are these so-called witnesses?" asked Red Stranger.

"Never mind them. We have enough evidence against this boy, so we don't need any witnesses to testify," Judge Davidson answered.

"What might that be?" inquired Red Stranger.

"That's not for you to know, but I'm going to see to it personally that you get sent away for a very long time. That ought to teach you not to break the law," Judge Davidson replied.

"Well, then in that case, make sure that my cell is to my liking. Otherwise, I will start a riot and break out before anyone can see me do it," Red Stranger told him.

He then began to count something on each of his fingers.

"What are you doing now?" asked Judge Davidson. "I'm counting the minutes until I exit—that is, if you don't mind speeding this up a little bit so we can be out before it gets dark," Red Stranger answered.

"You'll leave when I tell you to. Now sit there and be quiet. I'm starting to lose my patience with you," Judge Davidson told him. "I'd be careful if I were you and not lose my temper in front of all of these people. It would be bad for your image as a judge, as well," Red Stranger began.

"I don't want to hear another word out of your mouth unless I ask you a question or tell you to speak," Judge Davidson said. "You can try, but I will never be silent as long as I am on this earth and breathing. It wouldn't kill you to show a little sympathy for a poor boy," Red Stranger added.

"I'm getting very fed up with this boy's attitude and hereby sentence him to be relocated to the West Coast to do hard labor for seven years. After that, we can evaluate what to do with him next," Judge Davidson told them.

"Is that all you've got?" asked Red Stranger. "I can make your sentence much longer if you continue to be a nuisance in my courtroom. Now, don't say another word," Judge Davidson began.

"I'd like to see you or anyone else try and keep me quiet. I can tell you this right now: you wouldn't have much luck. And if I were to tell someone how I have been treated here today, they might have a thing or two to say about it and would make you all pay the price for your arrogant, corrupt, and hypocritical ways of doing things," Red Stranger said.

"Do you have anything more that you want to say?" inquired Judge Davidson. "Let me take a minute to think about that before I give you my answer," Red Stranger replied. "I have no more use for this boy. Bailiff, you can take him away now because I've had enough of his malarkey. We will have a five-minute recess then proceed with the next case. Court is adjourned for now," Judge Davidson told them as he banged his gavel on the desk.

"Come on, you," the bailiff urged. "Oh, I'll come, but I won't like it," Red Stranger added. He then got up from the stand and went with the bailiff back to his cell. As the people filed out of the courtroom, both Robert Porter and Doc tried their best to make their way through the crowd of people, but there was a lot of pushing and shoving going on.

"Aren't we supposed to get paid?" asked Robert Porter. "That was mentioned, but I guess it never happened. We don't have to do everything for money," Doc answered.

"I was hoping that we'd get paid. That was the agreement between us and Mr. Swindle, remember?" Robert Porter began. "Knock it off, Porter. Now that Stranger is gone, things will never be the same, and there won't ever be anyone like him again. And I don't care who knows it," Doc snapped, and they went back to the liquor store to report to the others about the trial.

When they got back to the liquor store, they hurried to the back as fast as they could because after Red Stranger had gotten caught, they were now more paranoid about being out and around people.

"What was the outcome of the trial?" inquired Albert Swindle. "It wasn't good. The judge came down hard on Stranger, and he's to be relocated to the West Coast to do hard labor for seven years," Doc replied.

"That's too bad, but it most likely will happen to us eventually. That's the sad reality of it and can't be avoided," Mr. Swindle told them. "It could happen sooner than you think, but that's why we have to take more precautions than before so we aren't next," Brock began. "If it's any consolation, we can figure out how to outsmart the police so that none of us get caught," Abigail said.

"That's not such an easy task. It may have worked for Stranger, but it might not for the rest of us. Some of them are tougher than others and don't take any kind of nonsense from anyone," Mr. Ferguson replied.

"How do we solve this problem?" asked Mrs. Porter.

"We'll have to think of something, but for right now, we shouldn't worry about it. Because this happened, we have to look after ourselves. Now, let's go, Mr. Porter and Mrs. Porter. We should be getting back to the caravan now because it's getting late," Mr. Swindle answered.

They then followed him back to where the caravan was parked. With Red Stranger gone, they would have to do their best to avoid the police as much as possible to escape the same fate. But with some effort, their chances would be much slimmer. They didn't dwell much longer on Red Stranger's departure and went on as if nothing had happened. Even though Doc was taking it the hardest, he didn't want to let it affect his time when he was out making money, because inside he knew that was what Red Stranger would have wanted him to do if he were the one to get caught.

Even though the month was just about to wrap up this week and the first of August happened to fall on a Thursday, Albert Swindle was in a major crisis. He was starting to run out of money again and had used half of it to bet on a horse race and lost. He barely had enough to feed the three children who were in his care, let alone himself. Mr. Swindle was getting really fed up with the mundane life that he was currently leading and didn't know how he could make some quick money so that he and his pupils could eat. Albert Swindle didn't care how he was able to do it, and when it came to matters about money, he would do whatever he had to just to get at least a little food to hold him over until he could somehow get more.

Mr. Swindle spent his nights in his room with a pad of paper and pen, writing down all the different ways he could make some money. He thought of selling his caravan but realized that if he did that, he would have no other place to live. Although Mr. Swindle would make enough money from it to have food for a whole month, he knew that he couldn't part ways with his collection of stuffed heads because he was very attached to them, being that his only hobby was taxidermy.

The next thing on his list was to give blood, which paid a good amount of money because blood banks were looking for people who would give their blood and get paid for it. But Albert Swindle was afraid of needles, and on top of that, he was squeamish and couldn't stand the sight of blood, so that was out too. Albert Swindle was starting to run out of ideas, and the ones on his list, he had to cross out a lot of them, so now it was down to four of his ideas. Mr. Swindle started to regret that he ever bet on that horse race, but he was confident that he would win for sure and was devastated when he found out that he had lost.

Albert Swindle had this narrative in his head to mug a random person and take their money and do it in a way that he wouldn't get caught by the police. It was becoming more and more crucial than ever. No matter what, Mr. Swindle had to do it, even if he had to resort to doing it in the way that the homeless people did to make money, then so be it. This internal dialogue made more sense than anything on his list. There was one thing that Albert Swindle wanted, and that was money, and he would get it no matter what it took.

CHAPTER 9

Unravels the Storyline of How Ezra Was Chosen to Do a Job for Mr. Albert Swindle

Another day had dawned, and with it came a deep depression that enveloped Mr. Albert Swindle. He wasn't his usual self, but that didn't stop his three pupils from diligently carrying out their daily work. The shortage of money was, of course, the root cause, with even his secret stash dwindling to only a few single dollar bills and a handful of change. Mr. Swindle hadn't engaged in any business dealings since his last show, which was only a few months ago but ended up as a total failure, damaging his reputation as both a businessman and a magician.

While his pupils were eating breakfast at the dining room table, Albert Swindle sat on the couch in the living room, silent. Eventually, he got up and walked over to Robert Porter. "I have a job for you, Mr. Porter—that is, if you're up to it," he began.

"Does it involve any danger?" asked Robert Porter.

"Not in the least bit, but I will pay you a little if you agree to do it for me. You would be helping not just myself but all of us," Mr. Swindle answered.

"Alright, I'll do it, but you must pay me this time. I won't work for free anymore, and you still owe me from the last job," said Robert Porter.

"I know that, but I promise this time, plus the money from the trial I meant to give you. Emotions were running high that day, and it completely slipped my mind. But I won't forget, just as long as you do what I ask of you, because there's no one else that I believe in more than you," Albert Swindle replied.

"I'll do anything for money. Can you elaborate more so I can understand exactly what the job entails? I don't do anything that involves heights or insects," added Robert Porter.

"Do you know that homeless girl?" inquired Mr. Swindle.

"Yes, but she's not my type, if that's what you're implying," Robert Porter replied.

"No, it's nothing like that. I want you to spy on her, everywhere she goes. You must follow and report everything back to me so I can pass it along to Mr. Ferguson," Mr. Swindle instructed.

"Is she having a problem?" asked Robert Porter.

"That's kind of it. I've been communicating with Mr. Ferguson, and he says that she's been acting very strange lately and wants to know why. That will be your job," Mr. Swindle answered.

"Why can't I do it?" inquired Mrs. Porter.

"Because we need two people for the work, and both Nathan and you are my special helpers, getting to do special jobs for me that I know you will be good at," Albert Swindle replied.

"What might that be?" Nathan asked.

"You will find out at the appropriate time, but now it's time for the three of you to get to work. Now go, and don't let me catch you goofing off, or I will deduct it from your pay," Mr. Swindle answered.

And the three children got up and went to start their work without finishing their breakfast first. Nathan had to clean the tires of the caravan without any help, while Robert Porter and Mrs. Porter worked inside, sweeping and mopping the floors. Once they finished, Albert Swindle came to inspect their work.

"We're all finished, Mr. Swindle, sir," Robert Porter began. "Nicely done, you two. Now, the next thing that I need you to do is sort through all my travel magazines that I have in my closet in my room. You can also rearrange them by each monthly issue," Mr. Swindle said.

"In what part of the closet are they?" inquired Mrs. Porter. "They're all the way in the back, behind my clothes. There's a lot of them, so maybe you can throw some away, as well, so that I don't have such a big clutter in my closet," Albert Swindle replied.

"Why do you make Nathan do it instead of us?" asked Robert Porter.

"It's because I have the utmost faith in the two of you, and not Nathan. He's a good and hard worker, but he's nowhere near yours and Mrs. Porter's level. That's why I know that I can count on both of you more than I can with Nathan. He's never had that much motivation to do anything other than the work that I've given him to do," Mr. Swindle answered.

Just then, Nathan went into the caravan. "I'm done with the tires," he told them.

"Excellent job, my boy. Your next job will be to clean the dining room table. The glass cleaner is underneath the sink, and you already know where to get another rag. And when you are finished with that, your next task will be to clean out the refrigerator and to clean the sink in the kitchen," Albert Swindle told him.

"Which should I do first?" inquired Nathan.

"Whichever one you want, but I want my caravan to be completely spotless, both inside and out. Remember, presentation is everything and what matters the most. All of you, get working. I don't have all day," Mr. Swindle replied.

Then Robert Porter and Mrs. Porter went into Albert Swindle's room as Nathan discarded his old rag for a new one and, after getting the glass cleaner, began to clean the dining room table. The three children worked diligently until it was lunchtime. While they were eating, Mr. Porter got up from the table and approached Albert Swindle.

"Mr. Swindle, sir, I don't mean to bother you, but I was just wondering something," Robert Porter began.

"What is it, Mr. Porter?" asked Albert Swindle.

"I remember you saying that you need an assistant, so maybe you could train me. I can still sometimes pitch in with the work when we're not doing any shows," Robert Porter answered.

"To be perfectly honest with you, Mr. Porter, you are a hard worker and a great asset to my business. But I think it's best that we wait a little while longer until I have the time to train you properly first. And that takes time," Mr. Swindle said.

"Why can't you just start training me now?" inquired Robert Porter.

"My answer stays the same. Since I haven't done any shows for a long time, I don't need an assistant right now. But if I do down the road, then perhaps I can use you," Albert Swindle replied.

Robert Porter made a face to show his disappointment and then went and sat back down with Nathan and Mrs. Porter to finish eating his lunch. "Are you finished eating yet?" asked Mr. Swindle. "I am, but these two may need another minute," Nathan answered.

"You won't have time to finish now. Get back to work before I make the three of you wash my clothes the old-fashioned way. You already know what it is that you have to do," Albert Swindle replied. The three children just stayed seated and looked puzzled. "What do you want us to do?" inquired Nathan.

"I made a list of your daily tasks so that from now on, I don't have to tell you all the time," Albert Swindle answered, holding up a sheet of paper with writing on it. He then put it on the table in front of them. There were three columns that had each name on it and had different tasks. They each read theirs in the order that put them in by the hours of the day.

"Why do I have to be the one who washes the tires?" asked Mrs. Porter. "I gave that job to you for a good reason and will tell you what it is later on today in my room," Mr. Swindle replied. "You should consider yourself lucky. I have to be the one who always has to sweep and mop the floors in here," Robert Porter replied.

"What's on that list is final. Now, go to work and share that list amongst yourselves because I'm not making any copies," Mr. Swindle told them. It was then that the three children got up from the table and went back to work. Once they were all finished for the day, it was dinnertime.

"I don't know how much more I can take of doing this manual labor every day," Robert Porter began. "What do you mean by that?" inquired Mrs. Porter.

"Isn't it obvious? Swindle is making us be his slaves. He'll never make me his assistant. It's all an act. I should have never agreed to come work for him in the first place. I would be better off doing what I want to," Robert Porter said.

"What was that, Mr. Porter?" inquired Albert Swindle. "Nothing, sir. I was only joking around. I like working for you. I'm being honest and wouldn't want to be employed with anyone else," Robert Porter answered. Mr. Swindle gave him a stern look then went back to what he was doing before. The three children sat there silently, not knowing what to say about what just transpired.

"Are you trying to get all of us into trouble?" asked Nathan. "I'm telling you the truth. Swindle is using us. Whether or not you want to believe it is up to you, but I won't stick around here much longer and be forced to break my back every day just to make a little bit of money," Robert Porter replied.

"You're not the only one who thinks that. I, too, want to be free of this, but it's not that easy to do. Because if we were to do that, Swindle has his ways of finding us," Nathan answered.

"How would he be able to do something like that?" inquired Robert Porter.

"We should listen to what he says, Robert dear, and shouldn't underestimate someone like Mr. Swindle," Mrs. Porter answered.

"Do you know what the repercussions would be?" asked Nathan.

"No, and I don't really care. If Swindle does somehow track me down, I'll just get away again. But this time, I'll do it so he won't be able to ever find me, because anything is better than having to stay here and suffer," Robert Porter said.

"Why can't I come with you?" inquired Mrs. Porter.

"Because Swindle will have your head, too, if he knew that both of us got away. And knowing this little weasel, he would probably snitch on us so that he can laugh in our faces while we're getting a beating from Swindle," Robert Porter answered.

"Do you think I'd snitch on you two?" asked Nathan.

"If you were forced to, like, let's say that Swindle threatened you, then you would crack under pressure and give away where we are. Then we would be in hot water with Swindle, and we'd have you to blame for it," Robert Porter replied.

All of a sudden, Mr. Swindle came into where they were. "What were you all talking about?" he inquired.

"Nothing that's important, sir," Nathan answered. "Start getting ready because we have to go somewhere soon and need to be on time," Albert Swindle told them.

"Where are we going?" asked Mrs. Porter.

"You'll find out when we get there, but I need the three of you to go out back and wash yourselves off with the hose. Get all the dirt and filth off of you first," Mr. Swindle replied.

"It was at that point that the three children got up from the table and went outside to the back where the hose was set up so that they could wash themselves off. When they were done doing that, they came back inside. Albert Swindle took the caravan over to where Red Stranger's spot was, which was now occupied by Doc. Once there, they saw that both Brock Ferguson and Abigail were already there. They were sitting on the chairs while Doc sat up against the wall where he slept.

"You shouldn't be here, Swindle. It wasn't very smart of you to think we should meet now, of all times," Mr. Ferguson began.

"I just wanted to come see you and also see how you're doing. But from the looks of it, not so good," Mr. Swindle said.

"He hasn't been feeling well lately and doesn't have any insurance or money to go to the doctor," Abigail replied.

"What did I tell you about telling other people my business?" inquired Brock.

"I can see that you're ill, but that shouldn't stop you from doing what you always do. Maybe it would be smart to get some over-the-counter medicine that might help you get better," Albert Swindle added.

"Do you really think the great Brock Ferguson would take medicine?" asked Doc.

"Shut up, Doc, unless you want to be sick too. I can tell you it's no fun. I feel like I'm dying and won't ever recover," Mr. Ferguson answered. He then let out a loud hacking cough but tried his best to stifle it so that no one knew it was there.

"I hope you get better soon. Being sick can be tough and frustrating, but just hang in there, and you'll be back to your old self in no time," Mr. Swindle told him.

"Your positive pep talk makes me feel even worse than I already do, and I have trouble sleeping for the last two weeks because of this illness. If I don't get a full night's sleep soon, I'm going to go insane," Brock began.

"Take it easy, Brock. Maybe you should lay down and rest for a little while. It might do you some good," Abigail said.

"Don't patronize me, girl. It's bad enough that I'm sick, but I don't need anyone nursing me back to health. I can do that on my own," Mr. Ferguson replied. He then coughed again, harder than he had the first time, almost falling out of his chair.

"What are you going to do to make yourself better?" asked Doc.

"If I drink enough fluids and take care of myself, it should be another week or so before I should be well again," Brock replied.

"I really feel sorry for you, Brock, and I know you are going to get through this. Just be patient and keep your head up. You'll start getting better every day," Albert Swindle told him.

"What do you care if I get better or not?" inquired Mr. Ferguson.

"He's not the only one. I, too, am pulling for you, as is Doc," Abigail answered. "Speak for yourself. I'm just glad it's not me, because I get very irritable whenever I get sick, but that's extremely rare," Doc added.

"Keep out of this, both of you. I have to figure out a way to somehow get rid of this illness soon, but nothing I'm doing is working," Brock began.

"Did you try eating some hot soup?" asked Mr. Swindle.

"Don't be foolish, Swindle. I have no way of heating it up. Besides, I don't really care for soup all that much anyway," Mr. Ferguson replied.

"Do you want me to get you anything, Brock?" inquired Abigail.

"No, just leave me be, girl. This whole being-sick thing has been a total nightmare. I need to be well again because I'm losing money every day that I'm not on the medians or making deals with people," Brock answered.

All of a sudden, Abigail started to go somewhere, and Albert Swindle nodded to Robert Porter to follow her. "Where are they going?" inquired Doc.

"Don't worry about it. They'll be back soon enough," Mr. Swindle replied.

"If I don't regain my strength anytime soon, then I might as well catch up on my sleep until I'm able to go back to working again. That seems like the only thing that I can do right now," Mr. Ferguson told them.

"I have a good feeling that's what you need the most and will make all the difference in getting you one step closer to feeling good again," Albert Swindle began.

"Are you kidding?" asked Brock.

"No, my friend. I'm being completely serious. When a person is sick, that is something that usually helps," Mr. Swindle answered.

It was then that both Abigail and Robert Porter returned. "I have to talk with you, Mr. Swindle, sir," Robert Porter said. "Will you excuse us for a minute?" inquired Albert Swindle. "Don't be too long. I haven't finished venting to you yet," Mr. Ferguson replied. Mr. Swindle got up and took Robert Porter aside to hear his report. "What did you find out?" asked Albert Swindle. "She only went around the corner for a walk, and that was all. I followed her everywhere she went but gathered nothing to report yet," Robert Porter answered. "You're doing well, Mr. Porter, but you must keep on her and find out as much as you can. And when you do, you must tell me right away," Mr. Swindle added. "When do I get my money?" inquired Robert Porter. "As soon as you give me some information, then I will pay you. But not until then. We have to figure out what she's up to. That's what's most important," Albert Swindle replied. "Yes, sir, I will keep that in mind. Let's hope that there's something to report soon, and I won't let her out of my sight while we're around here," Robert Porter told him. "That's a good boy. Also, when you're doing that, you must keep out of sight. She is not to know you are spying on her," Mr. Swindle added.

They then rejoined the others. "Why don't you try to drink some orange juice?" asked Abigail. "No, I hate that stuff. It tastes disgusting, and I especially hate all of the pulp that is inside of it because it only gets in the way," Brock answered. "We should be going back to the caravan now. The hour is growing late. Come, my friends, you have to go to sleep so you are all rested for work tomorrow," Albert Swindle began. His pupils followed him back to the caravan.

Mr. Swindle wasn't completely sure, but he was starting to question Robert Porter's loyalty toward him and had a feeling that he might suddenly betray him. But it was only a feeling at that time, which came and went. However, he wanted to see how things would play out between them. Albert Swindle had bigger fish to fry. He wasn't going to spend too much time worrying that someone like Robert Porter would do such a thing.

Even though Swindle had little money, he hoped that they would have Trevor back in their possession and, afterward, that Trevor would be dead, and Swindle would have a lot more money. He was thinking of cutting down his shows to two or three days a week instead of five. With the money, the first thing that Mr. Swindle wanted to do was to stock up on boxes of cigars. That way, he wouldn't run out for a few weeks. He had taken up smoking to calm his nerves, and it worked. But what Albert Swindle wanted the most was revenge on Trevor. That was eating him up inside so much that he stayed up half the night until he finally fell asleep. Even when Swindle lay in his bed, that was all he thought about.

Through some twist of fate, Mr. Swindle had had enough of feeling like a total failure and wanted to go back to being on easy street again as he had been before Trevor had jinxed him, or so Albert Swindle believed. He became more and more anxious each day, pacing the floor of his room like a caged animal just waiting to be released so that he could make Trevor pay and get the money. When that happened, Mr. Swindle looked at it as though when the smoke had cleared, he would have gotten his revenge and more money. Only then would Albert Swindle finally be able to rest easily again.

CHAPTER 10

A Secret Midnight Gathering

By some rather unusual obscurity that was now taking place around the homeless people who wrestled with the strange behavior of Abigail, they were starting to think that she might have a nervous breakdown at any time and would have to take a sabbatical from her regular life to find some sort of inner peace. That might help her snap out of whatever it is that had been bugging her. The truth was that out of the goodness of her heart, she wanted to help make sure that Trevor came to no more harm from anyone, and it was the right time to find a way to get herself all the way from Miami to Norman's house so that she could inform them about the wicked plot, which had been formed by none other than the criminal mastermind, Mr. Albert Swindle, himself, with Spyder's involvement, as well.

The day started out sunny, but then the rain came in the afternoon as it always did. But it came down so hard that even the wind blew harder, as if there was a hurricane going on. As the storm raged outside, Trevor and Rhonda were in the living room, working on their no-sew fleece blankets, which they bought at a craft store to give them something new to learn, and it was very time-consuming.

"Did I do this the right way?" asked Trevor, looking at the knot that he had just made in his blanket.

"You almost got it, but you just tied it too many times. I will help you in a minute when I finish with this knot," Birdie answered.

"I can't wait until my blanket is all done; I want to use it tonight when I go to sleep. It looks so cozy and comfortable," Trevor began.

"It's really coming down out there. It's a good thing we decided not to go out today. Otherwise, we might have gotten caught in this storm," Rhonda said, looking out at the window at the thunderstorm.

Just then, Margaret appeared. "Those are really looking good," she told them.

"Are you still cleaning out the garage?" inquired Birdie.

"Yes, but I'm almost done. You wouldn't believe all the stuff I found in there, and there's so much dust everywhere that I couldn't stop coughing and sneezing. But I did manage to throw out a lot of things in plastic bins that were broken and needed to be tossed out, and there's still more in there that I have to do," Margaret replied.

"Do you want me to help you?" asked Rhonda.

"If you don't mind, it's too much for me to handle on my own, and it would get done a lot quicker if we did it together," Margaret answered. "Can I help too?" inquired Trevor.

"Yes, with the lighter things, you can go through the stuff and sort it out for me. That would be very helpful. But first, you should finish your blankets. I better get back to work. Come and help whenever you get done," Margaret replied.

After Birdie and Trevor had finished their blankets, they went into the garage to help Margaret clean it out. While they were working, Trevor found something that he didn't recognize. "Look what I found!" he shouted. Margaret and Rhonda stopped what they were doing and went over to him. "Do you remember these, Birdie?" inquired Margaret. "No, I can't say that I do. However, they do look somewhat familiar to me, especially the yellow-and-blue one," Rhonda answered.

"We made these at summer camp. I did this one, and you did those two. It's hard to believe that we were so bad at arts and crafts that all of the other kids made fun of us," Margaret began. It was then that the door opened, and Norman stood there in the doorway, looking befuddled. "What are you all doing in here?" he asked.

"We're cleaning out the entire garage, as you can see. Margaret started it on her own, and before we came to help, Trevor and I made those no-sew blankets that we bought at the craft store," Birdie replied. "I'm starting to get hungry, so you and Margaret should start making lunch for us all and can finish cleaning afterwards," Norman said.

"Alright, but first let us get all cleaned up, then we'll get right on that," Rhonda replied. "What are we going to have?" inquired Trevor. "Whatever is in the freezer hasn't been used yet. I think I saw some chicken cutlets in there a few days ago. That's something that we can cook," Margaret answered.

They then all went out of the garage and back into the house. Since they got a late start on lunch and since it would take some time before it was ready, Trevor assisted Norman in rearranging the books in his office. This was because he wanted them to be in alphabetical order by the authors' last names. "Where is that Civil War book?" asked Norman. "I think it's somewhere over there, sir. I may have seen it," Trevor replied.

"We have to find that one because it's the one that comes next and is also very sentimental to me. I would not be happy if it was ever lost or stolen," Norman told him. "I can help you try and find it if you want me to, sir," Trevor added. "I would really appreciate it. You look in the pile that you thought you saw it in, and I will look in these two," Norman began, pointing to a giant stack of books.

They searched as hard as they could. "I found it, sir! It was just where I said it was!" Trevor shouted. It was then that Norman went over to where Trevor was, and he handed him the book. "Yes, this is the one I was looking for. You did well, Trevor. Now I can put this in a place where I know where it is and won't misplace it ever again," Norman said, and he then placed the book on one of the middle shelves.

"I would someday like to learn and read all about history because it sounds so interesting to me," Trevor replied. "That might be a little bit too advanced for you. I suggest you wait until you have improved your reading skills. There are a lot of big words in those books that you might not understand," Norman began.

Just then, there was a knock on the door. "Come in!" Norman shouted, and Margaret entered the office. "It looks like you're making a lot of progress with whatever it is that you're doing," she said.

"I was just helping Mr. Norman rearrange his books in here, but we're already halfway done and only have three more piles to do," Trevor replied.

"What is this book about?" inquired Margaret.

"That's one about how to start a financial career. Someone gave it to me, and I only read a little bit of it, but I am thinking of getting around to reading the whole thing," Norman answered.

"I just came to tell you two that lunch is just about ready, and you two should come in now," Margaret told them. Suddenly, Norman turned to Trevor. "I can finish up the rest of this after lunch. If you want to help Margaret and Birdie in the garage, then that's okay with me. But you don't have to make a decision right now. Let's just enjoy lunch," he said.

They then went out of the office and into the kitchen, where both Trevor and Norman sat down at the table. "Do you two like apple pie?" asked Rhonda.

"Yes, I do, especially when it's hot and fresh," Norman replied. "I can't say that I've ever had a pie before, let alone one made with apples, but I do want to try it," Trevor began.

"That's good to know because I baked one for us to have for dessert after we're done eating lunch," Margaret said. "What smells good?" inquired Trevor.

"That must be the chicken cutlets. We are also having mashed potatoes and green beans, but they should be ready soon," Birdie replied. She then carried the plate of chicken cutlets over to the table and put it in the middle. There was, at that moment, a dinging sound coming from the oven. "Can you take the mashed potatoes out of the oven?" Rhonda asked Margaret.

"Yes, but I can't seem to find where the pot holders are. They were just here a few minutes ago," Birdie answered.

"I left them over by the sink," Margaret told her. She then went to check on the green beans. "Did it stop raining yet?" inquired Norman.

"I can't tell. It's cloudy, but it looks like it's only drizzling now," Rhonda replied. After they were done eating lunch, both Margaret and Birdie went back to cleaning out the garage, while Trevor helped Norman finish rearranging his books.

By the early evening, they had a late dinner because they had only had lunch a few hours ago. Trevor found in Norman's office a *National Geographic* magazine that was about life in Africa. Trevor took it with him to his room, but while looking at the pictures, he fell asleep. Norman, Margaret, and Rhonda were about to go up to their room, when they heard an unexpected knock at the door.

"Who could be coming over this late?" asked Rhonda.

"I don't know, but I will go see who it is. You two go upstairs and rest," Margaret answered.

Norman and Birdie went up to their rooms while Margaret went to answer the door. She slowly opened it, only to see Abigail standing there. "Is this the residence of Norman Kingsley?" inquired Abigail.

"Yes, but my uncle is resting now and wouldn't want to see someone like you," Margaret replied.

"I must speak with him. It's very important that I do. Please go get him," Abigail began.

"I already told you he can't see anyone at this time, so if you would go back to wherever it is that you come from, that would be most appreciated," Margaret said.

"I'm not leaving here until I talk to Mr. Kingsley. Even if I have to stand here all night and wait, then I will do that," Abigail replied.

"Look, my uncle doesn't do business with anyone of your kind, nor do we want to. So whatever you have to say, we're not interested in hearing it," Margaret told her.

"If you won't let me in, then I will come in to speak to your uncle. Then I'll come in anyway. But you're not going to get rid of me so easily," Abigail began, then she pushed her way past Margaret to go inside the house.

"I demand that you leave this instant before I call the police and have you arrested for trespassing," Margaret said.

"Where is Mr. Kingsley?" asked Abigail.

"I cannot tell you that. Now leave, and if you don't, then I will be on the phone with the police," Margaret answered.

"I'm not going anywhere until I speak with Mr. Kingsley. Now tell me where he is right now!" Abigail shouted so loudly that both Norman and Rhonda went out of their rooms.

"What's the meaning of all this shouting?" inquired Norman.

"This woman says that she needs to speak with you, but judging by appearance, it's probably nothing too important," Margaret replied.

"What are you here for?" asked Birdie.

"I have come to deliver some information to you regarding Trevor Conway. If you let me stay, I can give you more details on it," Abigail replied.

"Why should we listen to you?" inquired Margaret.

"Don't be rude to our guest. We must give her a chance to explain herself before we cast her out into the streets where she dwells," Norman answered. It was then that Norman and Rhonda went back downstairs.

"Let's go in the living room, and you can tell us more about what it is that you know," Birdie began.

They then all went into the living room to listen to what Abigail had to tell them. "Won't you sit down?" asked Birdie.

"No, I much rather stand because I can't stay for too long. I just came here to tell you that a villainous man named Albert Swindle is planning to get revenge on Trevor. He is conspiring with a man named Spyder and someone else who is like me," Abigail replied.

"How do you know this?" inquired Norman.

"I heard them talking about it. I hid away so that they didn't know that I was listening, but you must believe me when I say that Trevor could be in grave danger very soon," Abigail answered.

"What's your name?" inquired Margaret.

"Abigail. I know that you must look down on me for what I am, but I come from the goodness of my heart to warn you about this evil conspiracy that is going to take place," Abigail answered.

"We had heard Trevor speak the name of this Albert Swindle person, but this is the first time that we're hearing about someone named Spyder," Norman said.

"He's someone who you wouldn't believe would want to harm Trevor, but he has a reason behind it that even I was in shock when I heard it. But I cannot tell you it at this moment. Meet me down in Miami near the Biscayne Bay at midnight, and I will tell you more. Now, I must be going, for if the man who is like me found out that I was here, he would be the death of me. Thank you for listening, and goodbye," Abigail told them, and then she started to leave.

It was then that Rhonda took out some money from her wallet. "Won't you take some money so that you can get yourself something?" she began. "No, I don't want your money. Don't forget to meet me at midnight tonight, and please don't be late," Abigail said, then she left.

"Should we trust her?" asked Margaret. "I say yes, but we should still stay alert in case she is lying to us about the whole thing and is really using it to mug us," Norman replied.

"I don't think someone like her is like those that she associates herself with, because she seems honest and truthful to me," Birdie told them. "Let's hope you're right. Those sort of people can be unpredictable at times and using deception and persuasion to gain what they want. So if she is telling the truth, then we will discuss what to do," Norman added.

"What about Trevor?" inquired Rhonda. "Oh yes, one of us has to stay with him while the other two go meet with this vagabond woman," Margaret answered. "Which one of you wants to go with me?" asked Norman. "Since the meeting is at midnight, and I'm already starting to get tired and was thinking about going to sleep soon, you and Margaret can go and tell me all about it in the morning," Birdie replied.

"Alright, but if we don't make it back, then send out a search party to try to find our bodies," Norman began. "Don't say such a thing. We will just be safe when we go," Margaret said.

"What time is it?" asked Norman. "It's almost nine o'clock. We have a few hours until we have to leave, but we should probably go a little earlier because it will take us an hour to get down to Miami," Rhonda answered.

"Yes, but we still have some time until we're on the road. I think I'll go to my office because I have some work that I have to do," Norman said. "I'm going upstairs to my room to go to sleep. Goodnight, Uncle Norman and Margaret. Please keep yourselves safe. I want to hear all about it tomorrow," Birdie replied, and she then went upstairs to her room to go to sleep.

When it was close to midnight, Norman and Margaret got on the road to Miami. There wasn't any traffic. When they got there, they waited for Abigail to show up. "Where is she?" inquired Margaret. "I'm sure that she will be here soon. We just need to wait and be patient, and hopefully, she'll show up and isn't playing us for a fool," Norman replied.

"Wait, I think I see someone coming!" Margaret shouted, pointing afar to something that was going toward them. Sure enough, it was Abigail. She strode up to them. "Where's the other woman?" she asked. "She's at home with Trevor now. Please tell us more about what you were telling us earlier," Margaret answered.

"Alright, the three people involved in this plot are Albert Swindle, Spyder, and a man named Brock Ferguson, who I've known for a long time. They want to kill Trevor because his parents left a will before they died and left the money to Trevor. Spyder wants the money for himself and is going to split half of it with Albert Swindle and Brock once Trevor is finally dead. I could never forgive myself if that were to happen," Abigail told them.

"Can you tell us more about Albert Swindle?" inquired Norman.

"He's a very bad man who employs runaway children to do his bidding by making them work for him doing manual labor for very little money. Believe me when I say that my intentions are good, and I want both Albert Swindle and Spyder to finally get what's coming to them. Then we can all rest easily," Abigail replied.

"What about the other person that you mentioned?" asked Margaret.

"He's someone that I fear and hope that he never finds out about this meeting, or it will only turn out bad for me in the end," Abigail answered.

"What are they plotting to do?" inquired Norman.

"From what I know, Albert Swindle wants revenge on Trevor and has recruited the help of Spyder and Brock. I heard what it is they are going to do, but I shouldn't tell you because it's very despicable," Abigail answered.

"Is there a certain reason why?" asked Margaret.

"Like I said before, I can't tell you. Now I have to be going, for if the man who I spoke of was to know that I was here and giving you all this information, he'd have me killed for it. Please heed my warning for what I say the truth. Goodbye," Abigail replied, and then she hurried off and got onto a public bus.

Lurking nearby was Robert Porter. He had heard the whole thing and ran back to tell Mr. Swindle. It was then that Norman and Margaret started their journey back home. Now that they partially knew what the three menacing foes' scheme, they would have to sit down together and think up ways to thwart Albert Swindle's conspiracy. Even though the rest was shrouded in mystery to them, they knew that they had to put safeguarding Trevor as their number one priority. It was even more pivotal than it ever had been. They couldn't let Trevor's safety be compromised and needed to take whatever measures they had to just to keep Trevor, even if it took getting the police involved. What was unknown to them was that the villainous group was closing in and would soon finally put their plan into action, and soon, Trevor would unexpectedly find his way back into the hands of Albert Swindle.

CHAPTER 11

Unfolds the Plot of How Trevor Was Brought Back into the Clutches of Mr. Albert Swindle

The midnight gathering had served its purpose in some way, but there was still more to unveil. Summer was passing swiftly, and in the blink of an eye, the end of the month was nearing. Now that it was getting closer to the end of hurricane season, the rain started to decrease, but it still stormed every now and then. Gradually, it would soon be the holiday of Labor Day, marking the official end of summer for good. This was a relief because people were getting fed up with getting soaking wet and walking in puddles of water, which were slowly drying up, making it a little more tolerable to go places without having to worry about the weather conditions.

On that glorious morning, Norman and Trevor went for a walk around the neighborhood. They stopped to look at some of the different houses around then would continue. While they were walking, Trevor spotted a giant house that had two large black front gates. He stopped to admire it. "I bet that you would like to live in a house like that someday, wouldn't you?" Norman began. "Well, if you work hard in life, then you can enjoy life's luxuries."

"I hope that I can live in a house as big as that one someday. Then I would have rooms so that I can have company stay over," Trevor said. "Don't get ahead of yourself, my boy. It takes a long time for a person to be able to live in a house such as that, but it isn't impossible. Let's keep going," Norman replied, and they continued walking.

"I was thinking about something yesterday, my first trip to Miami, and how I was happy to be in a new city where no one knew who I was. But it felt like so long ago," Trevor added. "You mustn't think of that anymore. That was a different time in your life when you were more vulnerable because you had spent your life before that not knowing the dangers that are in this world," Norman told him. "It's not only that, sir. I was also thinking about my time with Mr. Swindle. He seemed like a kind man at first, but had I known that he wasn't, I would've never been with him," Trevor began. "Are you still worried that he might hurt you?" asked Norman. "Maybe a little bit. I don't think he would just move on so quickly and forget about me. He might appear at any time," Trevor answered. "I can assure you that he nor any bad person in this world can ever hurt you again, and you will always be safe when you're with me. Oh, look, there's our house," Norman said, and they walked past two more houses until reaching theirs. Trevor immediately went inside, while it took Norman a little more time.

"How was your walk?" inquired Margaret. "It was great. I saw so many big houses, and it was also good to get out of the house after being inside because of the rain," Trevor replied. "I'm so glad to hear that you enjoyed yourself. I'm making french toast for breakfast since we haven't had that yet, and I haven't had it since I was a little girl," Margaret told him. "Where's Rhonda?" inquired Trevor. "She's still asleep. She went to bed late last night, and I don't think we should wake her just yet. Hopefully, she will smell the french toast and wake up on her own," Margaret answered. "You're right about one thing: that does smell good. I sure can't wait to try your french toast," Norman added.

"I'm going to go wash up and sit at the table to wait until the french toast is ready. All that walking made me very hungry," Trevor began. He then went into the powder room to wash his hands before sitting down at the table. Margaret and Norman joined him, but they talked softly to each other so that Trevor couldn't hear their conversation.

"You want to go upstairs and wake up Birdie?" asked Norman. "If you're thinking that we should tell her about our midnight meeting with that Abigail woman, it's probably best to wait until Trevor is asleep. Then the three of us can discuss it. Oh, by the way, Mr. Greenfield called while you were out walking. He wants to come over for a visit later on today," Margaret replied. "I will call him back later after breakfast. I think I hear Rhonda. It looks like she got up just in time," Norman told her.

He was right because Birdie then went into the kitchen. "Good morning, everyone. Sorry I slept so late, but I was watching a very interesting documentary about the history of the Church of England, and it ended very late. I went to bed after it was over," she began.

"Do you want some french toast?" inquired Margaret.

"Yes, remember when Mother used to make it for us every Saturday morning when we were little? It's a good thing she taught you how to make it before she died. Otherwise, we would never have it ever again," Birdie answered.

After they ate breakfast, Norman went into his office to call back Mr. Greenfield. In the early afternoon, he came over for a visit. They spent the entire time in Norman's office. "You know, Victor, with the state election coming up, I have been very busy trying to get people to vote Republican because the current governor needs to go. He's done nothing to better our state. He has only made decisions that weren't good ones. And if the Republican candidate doesn't win, I swear I am going to move to another state," Norman said.

"Surely, you don't mean that. While I agree with you on some things, relocating may be taking things a little too far and might not make things any better," Mr. Greenfield replied.

"That kind of thinking is the reason why we have such lousy politicians in this state, because people can't see the truth and live in a delusional state where they think that things are what someone tells them even though it's really not," Norman told him.

"I couldn't agree more with you. If we are subjected to having to put up with another Democratic governor, I think I might start protesting until the next election," Mr. Greenfield added.

Just then, there was a knock at the door. "Come in!" shouted Norman, and Margaret entered the office with three books under her right arm. "I'm sorry to interrupt, but I found these books, and they are from the library. They are overdue and need to be taken back right away," Margaret began.

"Well, I'm way too busy to do it, so someone else will have to do it. If you have some time, then you or Rhonda could take them back," Norman said.

"You could send Trevor. This would be a good test to see if what I've been telling you is right," Mr. Greenfield replied.

"I think that's a good idea, but not to prove your point, but because he's the only one that can do it. Margaret, go get Trevor and bring him in here," Norman told him.

It was then that Margaret went to get Trevor, and in a few minutes, she returned with Trevor. "I need you to do something for me, my dear child," Norman told him.

"What do you need me to do?" asked Trevor.

"Those books that are on my desk are library books. They're overdue, and I have to pay the fee. But I can't go, and Margaret and Birdie can only go later," Norman began.

"I can do it if you allow me to," Trevor said.

"That's exactly what I wanted to talk to you about. The library isn't too far away, and I want you to go and return these books and pay the fee. Here is ten dollars that will cover the fee. Now go there and come straight back here," Norman replied. He handed Trevor a ten-dollar bill and then went over to his desk and handed him the books.

"I promise to be back in a few minutes," Trevor told him. Then he went out of the house and walked down the street. While he was walking, Trevor looked behind him and could have sworn that he saw Albert Swindle's caravan parked in the distance, so he started running very fast.

As he walked, Trevor had no idea that lurking nearby were Doc and Nathan, while Abigail went around yelling "Trevor, oh, Trevor! My dear son, where are you?" She then saw a policeman standing around and quickly went up to him. "What's the problem?" inquired the policeman.

"I am looking for my son. He ran away a few days ago. His name is Trevor Conway, and my husband and I have been worried sick about him," Abigail answered. "I will keep a lookout for him. In the meantime, you just continue to look, and I am sure that you'll find him," the policeman began. He then got into his police car and drove off.

Just then, she spotted Trevor going her way and quickly crossed the street but hid behind the bus stop. Trevor kept on walking and bumped into a punk skateboard kid who was riding down the street on his skateboard, almost falling off his board.

"Hey, watch it!" the punk skater kid snapped.

"I am sorry. I didn't mean to almost knock you over," Trevor said.

"Alright, but next time, try to be more careful, and watch where you're going," the punk skater kid replied, and he kept on riding down the street.

It was then that Trevor kept on going. Along the way, he saw some people dancing on the sidewalk, so he stopped to watch them. Suddenly, Nathan came up behind Trevor and tapped him on the shoulder. Trevor turned around and was surprised to see Nathan standing in front of him.

"What are you doing here, Nathan?" asked Trevor.

"I just wanted to go for a stroll, but there's something that I want to show you before I go," Nathan replied.

"I'm not going anywhere with you because you will just take me back to Mr. Swindle, and I don't want to see him ever again. Now go away," Trevor told him.

"That's just it. I am no longer with Swindle. I ran away from him because he's a bad man, and you were right about him," Nathan added.

"I still want to stay here. You can go if you want to, but I have to return these books at the library and pay the overdue fee," Trevor began.

It was then that Trevor kept on walking, looking back to make sure that Nathan wasn't following him. As he continued down the street, he was about to pass the bus stop behind which Abigail was hiding. Once he was close enough, Abigail jumped out from behind the bus stop.

"Oh, Trevor, there you are! I've been looking everywhere for you," she said.

"You really have?" Trevor replied.

"Yes, ever since you ran away from home a few weeks ago, I, your mother, have been worried sick about you," Abigail told him.

"Wait a minute. You're not my mother. I know who you are. You're Abigail. Leave me alone," Trevor added.

"How dare you call your mother by her first name? Now let's go. Dinner is just about ready," Abigail began. She then grabbed his arm and started to pull him.

"Hey, somebody help me, please!" Trevor started to shout very loudly, but it was no use. "Stop being so stubborn. We need to go home now," Abigail said, and she kept a hold on his arm even though Trevor put up a fight to try to make her let go. It was then that, out of the blue, Brock Ferguson appeared. He looked at Trevor with glee. "What's going on here?" he inquired.

"Oh dear, I found our son. Now we can be a family again. Now let's go home," Abigail answered. She still had Trevor's arm and was pulling him. "Let me go! These aren't my parents. My parents are dead. These are bad people! Please, someone help me!" shouted Trevor. But all those who saw what was going on just shook their heads in disgust and said, "What a naughty boy Trevor was," and they started walking.

Along the way, from out of nowhere came Doc, followed closely by Nathan. They continued to walk until they reached an area where no one was around, and there was Albert Swindle's caravan. They went up to it. The door then opened, and out came Mr. Swindle. He looked delighted to see Trevor.

"Why, if it isn't Trevor, my boy! We're so glad that you came back to us at last, and you look very well too," he said.

"Yeah, look at his fancy duds. He's a real gentleman, I would say. And look, he brought us some presents too," Doc added.

"What's that?" asked Albert Swindle.

"It's mine, Swindle," Brock said.

"No, it's mine, my friend. You may have the books because they're of no use to me," Mr. Swindle replied, and he swiped the ten dollars out of Mr. Ferguson's hand and gave him the books.

"I don't want the stupid books. Now give me back the money right now, or I'll take the boy back to where he came from," Brock began, and he then threw the books aside onto the floor.

"Alright, here, but consider this to be a gift of my generosity," Albert Swindle said, giving him back the ten-dollar bill.

"Oh, please give me back the money and the books. Otherwise, Mr. Kingsley will think that I stole them," Trevor pleaded.

"Of course, we will. We wouldn't want your friends to think badly of you," Mr. Swindle told him.

Trevor then turned to Nathan. "How could you betray me?" he inquired.

"It was just something that I had to do," Nathan answered.

It was at that point that both Robert Porter and Mrs. Porter went out of the caravan. "Well, if it isn't church boy. I bet you remember us and think that by running away, you had seen the last of us. Well, you're not the only one who got tired of that terrible foster home, and now we can finally get our payback," Robert Porter began.

"That's enough, Mr. Porter. You two have some more work to get done, so I suggest you get to it," Mr. Swindle said, and both Robert Porter and Mrs. Porter went back inside to finish their work.

"What should we do with him?" asked Doc.

"I say we kill that little brat and bury his body in a ditch somewhere," Mr. Ferguson replied.

"We can't do that. We must wait until Spyder gets here. I already contacted him, and he should be coming very soon," Albert Swindle told him.

"You're a lucky boy. If we didn't have to hold off, then I would kill you right here and now and make sure that no one would ever find your body," Brock added.

It was then that Mr. Swindle picked up a stolen golf club that was beside him. "You think you could get away from us and tell the police about us? Well, you are wrong," he began, and then he threw Trevor to the ground and started beating him with the golf club.

Trevor screamed in agony as everyone else watched in horror, but Abigail intervened and knocked the golf club out of Albert Swindle's hand. "Stop it, Swindle! Don't you lay another hand on that boy," she said frantically.

"Keep quiet, girl, and stay out of this if you know what's good for you," Brock replied.

"No, I won't do either, nor will I allow you to hurt him. And if you try, then I'll do whatever is possible to stop you, and don't think I won't," Abigail told him.

"Move out of the way, girl, or you'll be next," Mr. Ferguson snapped as he pushed her onto the floor. But she got right back up and positioned herself in the middle to protect Trevor again.

"I told you to stay out of it, girl. Now stop getting in the way," Brock added.

"I said no! Don't try anything, and keep away from the boy. You got what you wanted, now leave him alone!" shouted Abigail.

"Why, Abigail, my friend, it seems as though you care for the boy and are really an unlikely person to be a friend to him," Albert Swindle said.

"Strike me down if so. At least I am decent enough to actually show some compassion towards other people, unlike the rest of you brutes. I was very young when I got started doing what I am doing, and it may not be the most practical way, but I get by knowing that I have to. It works," Abigail replied.

"Abigail, my friend, we must be civilized when doing certain things," Mr. Swindle told her.

"Civilized, you say? The way I see it, this is far from it and more like you're intentionally ganging up on one person. There are other ways to handle things like this, but not the way you're doing it," Abigail began.

Everyone got really quiet until Albert Swindle was the first to speak. "Doc, go put Trevor in the cage that's in the corner of my room, and make sure that you lock it so that he can't get out," he said.

Doc then took Trevor by the arm and took him inside the caravan. He put Trevor in the cage and locked it, then he went out.

"Where did you get a cage from?" inquired Brock.

"I found it in the woods. I believe it's for a dog but thought that it would be of some use to contain Trevor," Mr. Swindle answered.

"You do always think ahead, that I will give you. But what I am more concerned about is that those people he was with finding out what we need and where we are so they can come and try to get him back," Mr. Ferguson told him.

"What makes you so sure that they will?" asked Albert Swindle.

"If they happen to get the police to help them, they can track our location very easily and be where we are faster than you think. That's why you should take your caravan to a place that they won't be able to find you," Brock replied.

"What's the use in even doing that?" inquired Abigail. "Unless you want to go to jail for kidnapping, we have to spread out in order to make it more difficult for them to track us down," Brock answered.

"Where are we to go from here?" inquired Doc.

"Back down to Miami, but we must stay low for now and will meet up again in a few days. But for now, I say farewell to you, my friends," Mr. Swindle replied. He went back into his caravan, followed by Nathan, and they started on their way down to Miami while the homeless people took the city bus back.

Trevor remained locked up in the dog cage in Albert Swindle's room. It was so cramped that he had very little room and had to position himself so that he was able to sleep, even though it was hard to. Trevor hoped that Norman and his two nieces didn't think that he deceived them, but he hoped that they would try to find him and rescue him from the evil clutches of Mr. Swindle.

It was then that Trevor started to cry. He mostly blamed himself for being too naive to believe that Nathan was ever going to change his ways. Trevor cried so much that it caused Albert Swindle to get annoyed with him and yell at him to stop. Trevor was given only a small piece of steak and juice that tasted bad because it was very watered down.

As the days went by, Trevor hoped that Norman and his two nieces were worried about him and didn't think any less of him because he disappeared all of a sudden with no explanation of why or where he went. Trevor knew that he had to wait it out, even though it seemed completely and utterly hopeless. He knew that all he could do was wait and hope that Norman and his two nieces would eventually come and save him.

CHAPTER 12

The Great Rescue

There was something about Trevor's strange disappearance that Norman couldn't wrap his head around. It was as though his friend had been right and telling the truth, that the whole thing had been a sham and that Trevor had done exactly what he said was going to happen. But in a way, Norman found that extremely hard to believe. He wanted to prove that Trevor had not just gained their trust only to end up deceiving them.

What was most baffling was that Trevor didn't seem like the type of boy who would do something dishonest on purpose. He wasn't a troublesome child who always made all the wrong choices as a part of his lifestyle. But then again, his friend Mr. Greenfield's point was valid; perhaps Norman didn't know Trevor as well as he thought he did. He didn't want to admit that he was taken for a fool just yet. He was going to give it some time first, and just maybe he'd be the one who didn't have to man up and admit that he hadn't been wrong.

Norman had recruited the help of the police, and he and Margaret stayed up all night trying to find out what had happened to Trevor. When morning arrived, both Norman and Margaret had gone out of the office looking worn out and with no energy. What they didn't realize was that it was actually a holiday. They were about to go into the kitchen to make a pot of coffee for themselves when Rhonda went down the stairs.

"Good morning and happy Labor Day to both of you," she began.

"What did you say?" asked Margaret.

"Today is the holiday of Labor Day, and we planned to have a barbecue to celebrate later on, remember?" Birdie answered. "We won't be able to have it because Margaret and I were up all night trying to locate Trevor," Norman said.

"Did you find out anything?" inquired Rhonda.

"No, so far the police have yet to find him, but they're working round-the-clock to try and find him. They have looked everywhere for Trevor, but there's been no sign of him anywhere," Norman replied.

"Maybe what we need is to go sleep since we were up the whole night and could really use a good rest to make us feel better," Margaret told him.

"Yes, I suppose you're right, but I can't help but worry about Trevor and hope that wherever he is, he's alright and not hurt," Norman added.

"Yes, I feel the same way. Until we find Trevor, I will continue to have anxiety until he is safely brought back to us," Birdie began.

"Oh, Mr. Greenfield called last night because he wanted to know if he could come over to visit you today, but we were so busy I didn't answer it. But he left a message on our answering machine," Margaret said.

"Well, even though I'm very tired, I think having him over will help calm my nerves about this whole thing with Trevor disappearing. I will call him in a few minutes," Norman replied.

They then had their breakfast, and afterward, Mr. Greenfield came over. "You look terrible," he told Norman.

"That's because Margaret and I were up all night. Let's go into the office, and I will explain everything to you," Norman added, and they then went into his office.

"Why on earth were you up all night?" asked Mr. Greenfield.

"It's because Trevor went missing yesterday. Neither I nor the police have been able to find him yet," Norman answered.

"See, I told you that boy was no good, but you didn't listen, and now you have to admit that I was right about him," Mr. Greenfield began.

"I will do no such thing. While you are entitled to your opinion, I suspect foul play is the reason for Trevor's disappearance," Norman said.

"Look, Norman, it's time to face the facts. He tricked you and isn't coming back, so it's best that you move on and forget about him," Mr. Greenfield replied.

"How could you say that?" inquired Norman.

"It all makes perfect sense. He was associated with some bad people who corrupted his mind to be like them, but he didn't want you to know until it was the right time for him to show his true colors. And that he went back to them, there's no other way to look at it other than that," Mr. Greenfield replied.

"You don't know what you're talking about. Trevor wouldn't get involved with them ever again, knowing that they treated him so badly and wouldn't want to go through that all over again," Norman told him.

"That's what he wants you to think, but really, that was just a made-up story that he had told you and your two nieces to cover up for what he was actually going to do. And that's not the truth. Then I will eat my words," Mr. Greenfield added.

It was then that the phone rang, and Norman answered it. After he was done, Norman looked as though he had heard some good news.

"Who was that?" asked Mr. Greenfield.

"It was the police. They were able to locate Trevor. Apparently, he was kidnapped while on the way to the library where I had sent him to return some books and pay the overdue fee. The kidnappers took him down to Miami, and we must leave at once," Norman answered.

He then jumped out from his seat and left his office to go see where his two nieces were. They were both washing the dishes from last night's dinner.

"You're never going to believe this, but I spoke with the police, and they were able to locate Trevor," Norman began.

"Where is he?" inquired Margaret.

"Down in Miami. He was kidnapped while on the way to the library, and we must go down there right away. There isn't a moment to lose," Norman answered.

"What about Mr. Greenfield?" asked Rhonda.

"I will have to cut our visit short, and he can come back in a few days, but this is more important. He already knows about it and understands completely," Norman replied.

It was then that Mr. Greenfield went into the room.

"I guess I should be going now. Call me later, Norman, and we can discuss when I can come and visit you again," he began, and it was at that point that he left.

Norman and his two nieces got into their car and drove down to Miami. When they got there, they didn't see anyone around.

"I don't like this. It seems like we're going to fall into a trap," Margaret said.

"They have to be somewhere. This was the location that the police had given me, but I don't think that they were wrong," Norman replied.

"Look over there. I believe that I see some people that might be them. Let's go over there," Birdie told them, and they went over to where the group of people were. Once there, they saw Brock and Doc standing there, but there was no sign of Trevor.

"Be careful, Uncle. These people don't look stable," Margaret added.

"Have you seen a little boy anywhere?" asked Norman.

"No, we don't know anything about no little boy. We're just standing here talking, that's all," Mr. Ferguson answered.

Suddenly they heard a muffled sound that was coming from nearby them.

"What was that?" inquired Margaret.

"It was nothing, probably just two animals fighting with each other. You know how they can be," Doc replied. They then heard the muffled sound again, but this time they recognized it to be Trevor.

"I know that voice anywhere. It's Trevor. You have had him this whole time. Let him go, or I'll call the police on both of you and have you arrested for kidnapping," Norman told them, and he started moving toward them but backed up a few steps because it was then that Brock pulled out a switchblade.

"Don't take one more step closer, or I'll cut you," he began. "Why did you kidnap Trevor?" asked Rhonda. "That's not for you to know, but we have him now, and he's staying with us, so you might as well just leave before you get hurt," Mr. Ferguson answered.

"How are we going to get Trevor back?" inquired Margaret. "We have to think of a way in which we won't get cut or killed," Norman replied. "Why don't we call the police?" asked Birdie. "Because that might only make him angrier. Perhaps I can do some negotiating with him, and we can make some kind of deal," Margaret answered.

"Whatever you're going to do, I hope that it works, because if not, then we're going to wind up in a life-threatening situation," Norman began. "What if we were to give you something in exchange for Trevor?" asked Margaret. "Unless you have something very valuable to give in return for the boy, then the answer is no," Brock replied.

"What if we were to give you some money?" inquired Rhonda. "That all depends on how much. If it's a little bit, then it's no deal. But let's say you give me two hundred, then I will give you back the boy, and you all can walk away unharmed," Mr. Ferguson answered. "I might have that. Give me a minute to look," Norman said, pulling out his wallet to see how much money he had in it.

"Don't try anything funny now. Remember, I still have the boy with me, and if you want him back and want to remain alive, then you will give me exactly what I want," Brock replied. "Here's your money. Now give us back Trevor, and be on your way. We don't have any more business with you," Norman told him, handing Mr. Ferguson the two hundred dollars, which he pocketed right away.

"Let the boy out of the cage. A deal's a deal," Brock ordered. "I think you got stiffed. No money is worth giving Trevor back. We took a lot of time to plan this kidnapping," Doc added. "Just do it already. We can't break the deal. They lived up to their end of the bargain. Now we have to do the same," Mr. Ferguson began.

Doc then went behind a tree, and after a minute, Trevor appeared. He started running toward Norman and his two nieces but was stopped abruptly by Brock, who grabbed him. "What is the meaning of this?" asked Norman. "If you really think that I would give you back the boy when our plan to kidnap him had succeeded, then you're wrong. We're keeping him and the money. So leave now, or else you'll be dead on the spot," Brock replied.

"That wasn't what we agreed on. You know that I gave you the money that you wanted. Now give Trevor back to us," Norman said. "The hell I will. He's never going to be with you ever again. So say goodbye to your friends, boy, because this will be the last time that you're going to see them," Mr. Ferguson replied.

"I didn't want to have to do this, but now it seems that I have no other choice. If you refuse to keep to our deal, then I will take drastic measures," Norman told him. He pulled out a small handgun and pointed it at Brock. Both Margaret and Birdie were very surprised by this unexpected turn of events.

"Come on, old man, do it if you have the guts to pull the trigger and kill me. If that's what it will take for you to get the boy back," Mr. Ferguson added.

"Why didn't you tell us that you brought a gun with you, Uncle?" inquired Margaret.

"It's because I figured that whoever the kidnappers are might be carrying some kind of weapon on them, and I wanted to be prepared in case I was right," Norman answered.

It was at that point that he lowered the gun. "What did you do that for?" inquired Rhonda. "I don't think that shooting him would solve anything. We will just have to think of another way to get Trevor back without resorting to murder," Norman replied.

"You're foolish to lower your weapon, but that gives me the chance to end all three of you for good," Brock began.

"What else do you want from us?" asked Norman.

"That's just it, I don't want anything else but for you to go away so that the boy can be where he belongs," Mr. Ferguson answered.

"If by that you mean with you, then I beg to differ. No sweet and kind boy should ever be associated with vile scum such as yourself," Margaret said.

"I've just about had it with you three meddling into my business, which is why I'm going to count to ten, and if you don't leave by then, then I will kill you," Brock replied, and he started counting out loud. But Norman and his two nieces didn't move.

When Mr. Ferguson got to ten, he threw Trevor down on the ground and ran with his switchblade toward them, while Doc hid behind the three where the cage was that Trevor was in. They scattered in different directions and were able to outsmart Brock. "I got Trevor, let's hurry!" Margaret shouted, and they ran as fast as they could back to their car with Mr. Ferguson not too far behind them.

Once they got to the car, they got in and quickly drove off. While on their journey home, Trevor was still shaken up from the whole experience. "Can you tell us all that happened?" inquired Margaret.

"While I was walking to the library, I ran into that boy Nathan. If you remember, he was the one who came to the window that time to tell us about what Mr. Swindle had planned. He tried to take me somewhere, but I refused to go with him and was able to get away," Trevor replied.

"I knew that boy wasn't to be trusted. He seemed like the kind of child that would make us believe that he was going to change his ways, but I had a feeling that he wasn't telling the truth about that," Birdie told them.

"What happened then?" asked Norman.

"I then ran into Abigail. She pretended to be my mother. I resisted her for as long as I could until that man and Doc showed up, and they brought me back to Mr. Swindle, where I was locked in a tiny cage in his room. But a few days before you came and rescued me, I was given over to that man. I don't know what happened to Mr. Swindle; he just disappeared," Trevor answered.

"We'll find him and the others who are working with him and bring them to justice. But the only thing that matters now is that you're safe and unharmed," Norman added.

"How were you able to find me?" inquired Trevor.

"We recruited the help of the police. They worked nonstop to figure out where you were located. In fact, my uncle and Margaret stayed up all night last night on the phone with the police. I would have stayed up with them, but I ended up falling asleep," Rhonda replied.

"Where is the money and the books?" asked Margaret.

"The bad people took them from me. I begged them as much as I could to give them back, but they wouldn't," Trevor answered. He was about to say something else, but all of a sudden, he fell asleep.

"Do you think that we'll be able to round up all of these bad people?" inquired Birdie.

"Yes, I'm sure of it. But this Swindle man is who we must find first. He is the one who is mostly behind all of this," Norman replied.

"Don't forget about that other man, Spyder. We haven't heard anything about him for a while, but he's somehow still a part of this," Margaret began. "Whoever he is, we have to find him as well as the homeless people who are involved in this plot," Rhonda said. "We already know that the man and boy have something to do with it, but with them scattered all over the place, it's going to take some time to track all of them down one by one. I will do everything in my power to make sure that they are all brought to justice, especially the fiend known as Swindle," Norman replied loudly.

"Keep it down, Uncle. We don't want to wake Trevor. He's been through a tragic experience, and the least we can do is let him get a well-deserved rest," Margaret told him.

"What about the woman who came to our house and we met with that one time?" asked Norman. "From what Trevor had told us, she helped in kidnapping him, so she's an accessory to the crime, too," Birdie answered.

When they had got home, Trevor woke up. He rubbed his eyes and slowly made his way into the house. He went right upstairs, changed into his pajamas, got into bed, and went back to sleep. He was just glad to be back with Norman and his two nieces. His back was hurting from having been in the cage for a prolonged time, and he had to sleep on his stomach, but the pain didn't go away.

In a way, Trevor felt like he had let Norman down by not making it to the library. Had he not stopped along the way, he might have avoided being kidnapped by the homeless people and taken back to Albert Swindle, which is something that Trevor never wanted. He also knew that even though he had once again gotten away from the bad people and that he hadn't seen the last of them, they would continue to terrorize Trevor. Because he had such a traumatic experience, just hearing the slightest sound made him cower in fear.

Trevor didn't like feeling the way he did and wished that he could go back to how things were before. But Trevor couldn't help but fear for his life, even though he knew that Norman and his two nieces would be on guard a lot more now, having the notion that the bad people might attempt to kidnap Trevor again or seriously harm him. Either way, it was a slippery slope that caused a lot of uneasiness. But regardless of this, Trevor wanted more than anything just to be reassured that he would never fall back into the hands of those who had done him wrong ever again.

CHAPTER 13

Brock Ferguson Finds Out Something Shocking and Takes Action

With Trevor back where he should be, everything seemed to be going back to the way it was; however, things were changing all around. Mr. Swindle had not been seen or heard from in weeks, and no one could get a hold of him. It was odd but possible that after the kidnapping of Trevor failed, he retreated somewhere to lie low for a while until all the ruckus had died down. It was presumed that Albert Swindle would reappear and that he didn't just disappear off the face of the earth. The question is when and where.

The homeless people had different thoughts on where Mr. Swindle might be, but a lot of them were far-fetched. They had a meet up every week, and in the absence of Albert Swindle, it was Brock who had taken up the role of temporary leader of their operation. That was only, of course, until Mr. Swindle returned.

Meanwhile, the homeless people were gathered to have their weekly meeting behind the liquor store. "What are we to do from here?" asked Doc. "How should I know? With Swindle missing in action, our operation is starting to fall apart, and if it continues like this, it's going to be impossible to mend back together," Mr. Ferguson answered.

"What do you suppose we do about it?" inquired Abigail.

"I have an idea. Let's just forget about everything and go back to our regular lives before we ever met Mr. Swindle," Doc replied.

"Did someone call my name?" asked the voice of Albert Swindle.

"I think our troubles are over," Abigail replied.

In front of them, Mr. Swindle appeared along with Robert Porter and Mrs. Porter.

"Where have you been?" inquired Brock.

"I was away for a little while because I needed to get away after the whole kidnapping plan failed. But don't worry, while I was gone, I was thinking of some new ways to make that boy's life a living hell. But first, my pupil Mr. Porter has something to tell you," Albert Swindle answered.

"I already told you what I heard. Abigail knew what was coming and, in a panic, was able to slip away before anyone could see her. Go ahead, Mr. Porter, tell Mr. Ferguson what you told me the other day."

"Abigail met with those people who Trevor is staying with, and she told them only part of what our plan is," Robert Porter began.

This infuriated Brock so much that he clenched his fist and it started to shake.

"I know you're angry, but you must control yourself. Otherwise, you might end up doing something crazy that could get you in a lot of trouble," Mr. Swindle said.

"Where is she?" asked Mr. Ferguson.

"She was just here a minute ago. I guess she was trying to save herself from facing your wrath," Doc replied.

"Shut your mouth, Doc! When I find her, I'm going to kill her! She thinks she can betray us, and if we ever find out, I want to know where she is right now! Someone better tell me or I'm liable to use one of you as a warm-up," Mr. Ferguson said.

"I know where it is that she went, but I might be wrong," Mrs. Porter added.

"Where did she go?" inquired Brock.

"I saw her cross the street, but that's all I know," Mrs. Porter answered.

It was then that Mr. Ferguson left and went across the street to find Abigail. When he got there, he looked all around but didn't see her, that is, until Brock spotted her and made his way up to her. When Abigail saw him, she tried to get away but couldn't because there was a wall in the way. Brock strode up to Abigail.

"Oh, hello, Brock. I was just going for a walk because I needed to stretch my legs a little bit, but I will be back over there in a little while," Abigail told him.

"You're really going to get it now, girl, so prepare yourself," Mr. Ferguson added.

"What did I do?" asked Abigail.

"You know what it is that you did, traitor. Everything you told those people was heard, and I am here to give you your punishment," Brock replied.

"No, please don't kill me, Brock. I didn't know what it was that I was doing. You have to believe me. I never meant to betray any of you," Abigail pleaded.

"Nice try, but you can't lie your way out of this. I can't just let you go scot-free. That wouldn't be right," Mr. Ferguson began.

He then grabbed Abigail by her dress and raised his shillelagh in the air, and then started to hit her with it until she was dead. Brock stood there with blood all over him and panting. He then picked up Abigail's body and tossed it into a nearby Dumpster. He began to walk with no particular place in mind, with Brutus following behind him. But as Mr. Ferguson was walking, he noticed that Brutus had stopped. Brock turned around quickly.

"What are you doing?" he inquired, but the dog just stayed where he was.

"Come on, Brutus, we have to go," Brock said, but Brutus still didn't move.

"Did you hear what I said?" asked Brock, but Brutus still didn't budge.

"So it comes down to this: my own dog has betrayed me too. I'm only going to say this one more time. Come on, Brutus," Mr. Ferguson told him, but Brutus remained where he was. Brock was now at his boiling point.

"Let's go, Brutus. Don't keep me waiting any longer!" Mr. Ferguson shouted, and he stomped his foot.

"Alright then, have it your way. Then I don't need you or anyone else. Just go find a different owner. But I have no time to stand around here," Brock began, and he turned and kept on walking until he was out of plain sight. Mr. Ferguson had committed a heinous crime, and all he could do now was go far away to avoid being arrested for murder.

Back at the liquor store, Albert Swindle and the others waited for Brock and Abigail to get back. When it got late, they started to worry.

"Where do you think Mr. Ferguson is? He's not back yet," inquired Robert Porter.

"I don't know. What could be keeping him? He left a few hours ago and hasn't been back. Maybe we should go look for him," Mr. Swindle replied.

"Where do you think he went?" asked Mrs. Porter.

"I bet he couldn't bring himself to kill Abigail and went traveling all around the country to find inner peace," Doc answered. Just then, Lola showed up.

"Where have you been hiding?" inquired Albert Swindle.

"I haven't. I've just been busy and went to a city south of here for a few months because I was barely making any money here," Lola replied.

"What's up with you?" asked Doc. "I was just going to go across the street because I heard that a new takeout restaurant just opened up, and I really want to try it," Lola answered. "You're on your own for that. We have other things going on right now that have to be taken care of," Mr. Swindle said.

"What do you mean?" inquired Lola. "It's not important; you go right on ahead. We have to discuss something together as a group," Mr. Swindle answered. "Suit yourself, but you're missing out. I'll be back in a little while," Lola told them, and she then left and crossed the street.

Lola got her food, and while she was walking back, she saw something hanging out of the Dumpster. She was curious about what it was and went closer. When she got there, she opened the lid of the Dumpster, and she was shocked to see Abigail's bloody body lying there. Lola let out a scream and ran back across the street.

Once Lola was back at the liquor store, she ran to the back and was out of breath. "What's the matter with you?" asked Doc. "I saw something in the Dumpster that you will never believe," Lola replied. "We can't guess, so just tell us," Albert Swindle added.

"Alright, I saw the dead body of Abigail. Someone murdered her and put her body in the Dumpster," Lola began. Everyone couldn't believe it; they were in a state of shock. "Are you sure that it was her?" inquired Mrs. Porter. "Yes, I'm positive. I just saw her a few hours ago, and for some reason, she seemed out of sorts about something, but I can't believe that she's dead," Lola answered.

"Do you think Mr. Ferguson was the one who did it?" inquired Doc. "I wouldn't be surprised. He was so angry that I can't think of any other person who would want to kill her," Mr. Swindle replied. "What if one of us is blamed for the murder?" asked Mrs. Porter.

"There's no sense in worrying about that right now because no one but Lola and us know about this, and it's going to stay that way. And if the police happen to question us about it, we will say that we don't know anything," Albert Swindle answered. "You do know that it's a criminal offense in this state to lie to the police. Even if we were able to make them believe that, it might come back to haunt us later on. And besides, they have no proof that I did it, so I have nothing to hide," Robert Porter said.

"No one ever got anywhere in this life from being honest, Mr. Porter. It's just a fact of life," Mr. Swindle replied. "What if someone were to find the body?" inquired Lola. "That's likely to happen since it's in a place where anyone can discover it, which is why we should probably go and retrieve it," Albert Swindle answered.

"Where are we going to put the body?" asked Mrs. Porter. "We'll decide that once we get the body out of the Dumpster. It's going to take three people to do it," Mr. Swindle answered. "Which of us should do it?" asked Doc. "Well, since we have three boys, we should be the ones who do it because it takes muscle and strength, which is something that we have that girls don't," Robert Porter replied.

"Who's the third?" inquired Lola. "I think he means Nathan. I will go get him right now, and the three of you can go together to get the body out of the Dumpster," Mr. Swindle answered.

He then went into the parking lot, where his caravan was parked. He explained the situation to Robert Porter and Doc. Together, they went across the street to retrieve Abigail's body from the Dumpster. Once they got there, Nathan opened the lid to the Dumpster. Flies were hovering all over the body, which smelled bad from having been in there for a few hours. It made Robert Porter cover his nose to avoid the rotten stench.

"How are we going to get it out of there?" asked Robert Porter.

"It won't be easy, but I think the best way is for someone to go into the Dumpster and pull it out. Then the three of us will carry it together," Doc replied.

"Who wants to be the lucky person?" inquired Doc.

"I think I'll pass. I'd rather not go in there and get garbage and blood all over my clothes, so it will have to be one of you," Robert Porter answered.

Nathan then turned to Doc. "Why don't you go in there?" he asked.

"Do you think just because I'm homeless, I wouldn't mind having to go into a Dumpster? But I draw the line at doing something like this," Doc replied.

"We're wasting valuable time. If you two won't do it, then I guess I have to," Nathan told them. He then climbed into the Dumpster and pulled out Abigail's dead body. Each of them grabbed a side and carried the body back across the street, taking a shortcut to avoid anyone seeing them.

When they had made it back to the liquor store, they put the body down onto the ground. "What should we do with it?" inquired Mrs. Porter.

"I think I have an idea. There's a canal not too far away from here. If we were to dispose of the body there, no one would ever find it," Albert Swindle answered.

"Alright, let's go do it then, because it's starting to smell worse, and I can't take it anymore," Doc told them.

"Not so fast. We have to make sure that no one sees us," Mr. Swindle added.

"What should we do?" asked Nathan.

"I know a way we can get to the canal without being seen by anyone," Albert Swindle replied, motioning them to follow him. The three boys carried the body, trying their best not to let the smell bother them, but it was so bad that they couldn't wait to finally be rid of the body.

When they got to the canal, they just stood there, waiting. "Alright, throw it in there," Mr. Swindle began.

"Shouldn't we say a few words first?" inquired Mrs. Porter.

"No, it would be better just to do it and get it over with, without any kind of formalities. It has to be done as quickly as possible," Albert Swindle answered.

It was then that the three boys picked up the body and threw it into the canal. Then they left to go back to the liquor store. "I still can't get over the fact that Abby is dead. She was always a good friend to me," Lola began.

"Where do you think Mr. Ferguson went?" inquired Doc.

"Probably somewhere far from here. We may never see him again, and if we do, we should keep our distance from him," Mr. Swindle replied.

"What if he were to show up here again?" asked Doc. "Then we would have to act natural, as if nothing had happened. We can't give him any kind of indication that we know what it is that he did, but I think we should now have a moment of silence for Abigail, even though she had betrayed us. It would only be right," Albert Swindle answered.

After the minute was up, they knew that they couldn't dwell on the tragedy any longer and felt it was best to move on. "I think it's absurd that we had to have a moment of silence for a traitor. She should have never done what she did but got what she deserved in the end," Robert Porter said.

"That's no way to talk about the dead like that, Mr. Porter. Yes, Abigail might have done it for many different reasons. She acted on her own, but that's still not a good excuse to disrespect the dead," Mr. Swindle replied.

"What should we do now?" inquired Mrs. Porter. "I think that it would be best if we let Mr. Swindle decide that now that he's the new leader," Nathan replied.

"As of right now, we have to be inconspicuous with this whole murder thing. It's the best thing to do. The police are everywhere now, and if they knew we were involved, then we'd all be up a creek without a paddle, and I'm sure you know what I mean by that," Albert Swindle told them.

"What if we were to use alternate routes when we go places?" asked Doc. "That wouldn't work because the police are all over this area, and if they were to spot one of us, then that would pose a major problem for us," Mr. Swindle answered.

Just then, they saw someone going their way. "Do you think that it might be Mr. Ferguson?" Nathan inquired. "I sure hope not. Otherwise, we better start running for our lives," Doc replied. As the person got closer, they were able to see that it was just Spyder.

"Why are you all so jumpy for?" he asked. "It's kind of a long story and something you would never have thought would have happened," Albert Swindle answered.

"Perhaps later, if I feel like hearing it, then one of you can tell me, but I've come back because I heard the kidnapping plan that Swindle came up with failed," Spyder began. "It wouldn't have if Brock hadn't let those people get the boy back. It's also Doc's fault, as well," Mr. Swindle said.

"Why is that?" asked Doc. "Because you left Mr. Ferguson high and dry when both of you were supposed to be in charge of the boy and to make sure that he remained with us," Albert Swindle replied. "I really don't care whose fault it is. All of you are incompetent fools. It seems that if I want something done, I should just do it myself," Spyder told them.

"What's our plan now?" inquired Nathan. "I don't know. At this point, it feels like we can't do anything without it getting thwarted, and I'm all out of ideas," Mr. Swindle answered. "Have you lost your mind, Swindle?" asked Spyder. "He does have a good point. If we are to make any sort of progress, then we have a strong and concrete game plan," Doc began.

"Does anyone have any suggestions?" inquired Mrs. Porter. But no one said anything. "It seems that we're stuck in a rut, and the only way to get out of it is to take some time to think things carefully. Perhaps if we do that, things will work out for us," Albert Swindle replied.

"There isn't any time to think. If we want the money, then we have to just wing it. That's the only way, and you know it," Spyder told him.

"I hate to say it, but you're right. That seems like the only thing that we can do now that might actually work," Mr. Swindle began. "Of course it will, provided that you all don't mess it up like you did the last time. I have to go because there's something else that I must do. I shall be in touch with you soon. Goodbye," Swindle said, and then he dashed off.

Now that they had a brand-new plan, which they believed was surefire, the question still remained if they could pull off whatever it was that they were going to do. With Brock nowhere to be found and Abigail dead, they had fewer people than before. However, that wasn't going to stop them from proceeding with what they were going to do.

Although they were apprehensive about the whole thing, they knew that this was what had to happen and that there was no other way. It was unknown how they were going to go about their newfound conspiracy, but if they were going to execute it and be triumphant this time, then they had to act as soon as possible because time was of the essence.

Now that Albert Swindle had returned, the group would have to make a few minor adjustments because of the tragic death of Abigail and Mr. Ferguson's unexpected departure. It was up to Mr. Swindle and Spyder to be the glue that held them together. They continued to have their weekly meetings, even though Spyder never attended any of them, leaving Mr. Swindle to be the facilitator. They also had to keep a low profile, which made it even more difficult for them to have meetings. It was beyond a shadow of a doubt that the group was confident that they were going to be victorious this time around because it wasn't just about the money anymore. They had some unfinished business and were determined to finish it.

CHAPTER 14

A Promise Kept

Twilight began to set in, and with it, the sun slowly rose over the early-morning sky. Eventually, it became completely light out, marking the arrival of another day. The radiance from the sunlight illuminated the tranquil blue sky, and people started waking up to begin their day. They enjoyed and couldn't get enough of the vitamin D from the plentiful sunshine, which made their mornings even more enjoyable.

It's not just these things that put people in a good mood when the day is new; some take a different approach, which is less cheerful. But no matter how a person decides to start their day, dawn is a time to celebrate a fresh start. For Trevor, this was particularly true because he was someone who really embraced it.

In the early part of the morning, the house was as quiet as could be. It wasn't until a little later that Margaret was the first person to awaken. She made herself a cup of coffee to wake herself up, then she sat on the couch while she sipped her coffee little by little. She couldn't help but wonder what psychological effect the kidnapping had on Trevor. Even though he seemed alright sometimes, Margaret could hear Trevor moaning in his sleep late at night, as her room was right next door to his.

The next one to awaken was Trevor, and he kept Margaret company until Rhonda woke up, and the two of them started making breakfast. It wasn't until eleven o'clock that Norman woke up. By then, breakfast was ready, and while they ate, Norman read the newspaper.

"What a tragedy that is," he began. "Is there something wrong?" asked Birdie.

"That homeless girl who we met and helped kidnap Trevor, her body was found in a canal down in Miami," Norman answered.

"Do they know who did it?" inquired Margaret.

"No, the police are still investigating, and the autopsy showed that she was murdered by being beaten to death with something hard," Norman replied.

"Are you saying that Abigail is dead?" asked Trevor.

"Yes, that was her name. It's very unfortunate, but she wasn't a good person, so in a way, it's not such a terrible loss," Norman answered.

It was at this point that Trevor started to cry uncontrollably.

"Why are you crying, my dear child?" inquired Norman.

"Because Abigail wasn't as bad as you think she was. I know she helped kidnap me, but she had a kind heart and was only trying to save me from going back to Mr. Swindle," Trevor replied.

"If you believe that was what she was going to do, her and her associates are all vile human beings with no compassion or empathy for anyone," Margaret said.

"Don't cry anymore. Whether or not she was trying to do what's right, we may never know, but that's no reason to cry over," Rhonda replied.

It was then that Trevor wiped his eyes with a napkin and continued to eat. "Does it say anything else about it?" asked Margaret.

"Yes, but I have to read the rest of the article later," Norman answered, putting the newspaper aside. Once they finished breakfast, it was half an hour until noon. Trevor was still upset over the death of Abigail, but he knew he couldn't make Norman or his two nieces see that she wasn't the bad person they made her out to be and that she wasn't like the others.

Norman shut himself in his office to read the rest of the article and the newspaper. While he was doing that, Margaret did a crossword puzzle in the living room, and Birdie did her daily exercises up in her room. By midafternoon, they had lunch. Norman went right back into his office again but eventually went out looking hysterical about something. He called up his friend Mr. Greenfield to come over, and they, along with Margaret and Birdie, all met in the kitchen.

"What's going on, Uncle?" inquired Margaret.

"I read in the newspaper that someone spotted Albert Swindle's caravan parked just down the street. He must be inside, and this gives us the chance to finally nail him," Norman answered.

"Where exactly is it?" inquired Margaret.

"It was seen in a parking lot of a shopping center. I will inform the police to meet us there, but we must go as soon as possible," Norman replied.

"Who's going to stay with Trevor?" asked Birdie.

"Both you and Margaret will stay behind while Mr. Greenfield and I go and capture Swindle," Norman answered.

"Do you think he has something to do with the murder of that girl?" inquired Margaret.

"I don't know, it's possible. He's one of the suspects. Come on, Victor, we have to get going before we're too late," Norman replied.

They then got up from the table. Norman called the police and, afterward, got into his car with Mr. Greenfield and went to the shopping center where Mr. Swindle's caravan had been seen. When they got there, Albert Swindle's caravan was parked. They surrounded it.

"Should we rush in and surprise him?" asked Mr. Greenfield.

"Yes, that might be the best thing to do. Let's go," Norman answered.

They barged into the caravan. It was pitch-black inside. They searched all over. "It's just as Trevor had described it to us," Mr. Greenfield told them. "We checked every room, and there was no one in them. I guess Swindle must have known we were coming and left his caravan here," one of the policemen added.

"He almost had him. If only we had come sooner," Norman began.

"How could he have known?" inquired Norman.

"Isn't it obvious? Swindle is wanted for the murder of that girl. Anyone in that kind of trouble would most likely disappear on purpose. But he won't be on the run much longer, that I can tell you," Mr. Greenfield replied.

"What should we do now?" asked another policeman.

"Let's get out of here. It's on us that Swindle was able to fool us the way he did, but hopefully, we'll get him next time," Norman answered.

They then left the caravan when Norman had gotten home after dropping off Mr. Greenfield at his house. He saw his two nieces standing in front of him; they looked eager to hear what had happened.

"Did you finally get Swindle?" inquired Margaret.

"No, we went to the place where the caravan was and even went inside but didn't find anyone," Norman replied. "That Swindle is a crafty fellow, but I know that if we're in the right place at the right time, we will get him and have him put away for good," Rhonda began.

"I wish that could happen sooner because I'm starting to wonder if we'll ever put an end to all this so that Trevor can live peacefully," Norman said.

"Don't talk like that, Uncle. We can't just give up. As long as Swindle is still out there, he can still try to harm Trevor. We have to think positively that we will get him, and when we do, we can all finally rest easily knowing that neither he nor any evil will ever be able to harm Trevor again," replied Margaret.

"What did you do while I was gone?" asked Norman.

"Not that much. I just did some dusting around the house. You'd be surprised at how much dust there is in this house, especially on the shelves," Birdie answered. "I did a couple more crossword puzzles before I decided to stop and rest. I also did some of my laundry because it needed to be done, and I didn't want to put it off until another day," Margaret told them.

"I think I will go into my office to read the rest of the newspaper. There are still a few more articles that I haven't gotten to yet," Norman began.

It was then that Trevor went into the room. "Where did you go, sir?" he asked.

"He just had to go run a few important errands that weren't that far away from here," Margaret replied.

"What are we having for dinner?" inquired Norman.

"Don't worry about that right now. We just ate lunch a few hours ago, but we are going to be making it in another two hours," Rhonda answered. "Well, I can't wait to see what the two of you are going to cook up, but I must get back to my reading before it gets late," Norman said.

"I found something in the upstairs closet, but I don't know what it is," Trevor replied.

"What does it look like?" asked Margaret.

"It's in a medium-sized tub and has little pieces that are different colors, and you put them together to make things out of them," Trevor replied.

"Why, my dear child, those are called Legos. They used to belong to Margaret and Birdie when they were younger," Norman told him.

"I think I will try and build something with them," Trevor added, and he went upstairs to get the Lego blocks from out of the closet. It was then that Norman went back into his office to finish reading the newspaper, and while he was doing that, both Margaret and Rhonda had some free time before they had to make dinner. It wasn't long before Norman came running out of his office. "What is it, Uncle?" asked Margaret.

"The police just figured out who it was who had murdered that homeless girl a week ago," Norman answered.

"Who was it?" inquired Birdie.

"If you remember, that man who had Trevor locked in a cage when we went to rescue him in Miami, it said his name is Brock Ferguson and also that the police are still trying to find him," Norman replied.

"He must have been working with Albert Swindle, but now that he's a fugitive, he must have cut ties with his associates and gone on the lam," Margaret added.

"Do you want to know how they found out it was him?" asked Norman.

"Yes, Uncle, please tell us," Rhonda answered.

"They found his fingerprints on her body, and that's how," Norman began.

"It does make sense, but what I'm trying to figure out is if he was the one who threw the girl's body into the canal," Margaret said.

"It's very likely that he didn't want anyone to find it, and that's why it was discovered where it was," Birdie replied.

"That's not all. The police also found fingerprints on the body that belonged to three different children, as well," Norman told them.

"Were they able to identify who they belonged to?" asked Margaret.

"No, the police tried to, but couldn't. All they were able to find is that the fingerprints came from male children," Norman answered.

"Do you think that boy who was Ferguson could be one of them?" asked Rhonda.

"Yes, I have no doubt about that. Clearly, he used them to do his dirty work, and that's how their fingerprints got on the girl's body," Norman replied.

It was then that Trevor went into the room. "What are you all talking about?" he inquired.

"We were discussing what we should have for dinner since it's going to be time very soon," Margaret answered.

"I made a building out of the Legos. It's in the living room and only took me a few minutes to make," Trevor added.

"We'd like to see it and will be there in a minute," Norman began.

It was at that point that Trevor went back into the living room. "Should we worry about this Brock Ferguson man being on the loose?" asked Rhonda.

"No, unless he happens to come here, then I think it's safe to say that we don't have to be the least bit concerned," Margaret answered.

They then went into the living room to see what Trevor had built with the Lego blocks. "What do you think?" inquired Trevor.

"It's very impressive, especially that you did it in such a short time," Norman replied.

"Thank you, sir. I really worked on it. I think that I'm going to make some other things, as well, because I have a few other ideas," Trevor said.

"You should get started on them right away, and after dinner, we can come back in and see what else that you made," Margaret replied.

"That reminds me, you and I should start making dinner now," Birdie told her.

"What do you have that we can make?" asked Margaret.

"I saw a few things in the freezer but couldn't tell what they were. I think the best way for us to decide is to pull them all out. We also have a couple of side dishes, as well, that we haven't used yet," Rhonda answered.

They then left and went into the kitchen.

"Who was it?" inquired Birdie. "If you remember, that man who had Trevor locked in a cage when we went to rescue him in Miami, it said his name is Brock Ferguson, and also that the police are still trying to find him," Norman replied.

"He must have been working with Albert Swindle, but now that he's a fugitive, he must have cut ties with his associates and gone on the lam," Margaret added.

"Do you want to know how they found out it was him?" asked Norman.

"Yes, Uncle, please tell us," Rhonda answered.

"They found his fingerprints on her body, and that's how," Norman began.

"It does make sense, but what I'm trying to figure out is if he was the one who threw the girl's body into the canal," Margaret said.

"It's very likely that he didn't want anyone to find it, and that's why it was discovered where it was," Birdie replied.

"That's not all. The police also found fingerprints on the body that belonged to three different children, as well," Norman told them.

"Were they able to identify who they belonged to?" asked Margaret.

"No, the police tried to, but couldn't. All they were able to find is that the fingerprints came from male children," Norman answered.

"Do you think that boy who was Ferguson could be one of them?" asked Rhonda.

"Yes, I have no doubt about that. Clearly, he used them to do his dirty work, and that's how their fingerprints got on the girl's body," Norman replied.

It was then that Trevor went into the room. "What are you all talking about?" he inquired.

"We were discussing what we should have for dinner since it's going to be time very soon," Margaret answered.

"I made a building out of the Legos. It's in the living room and only took me a few minutes to make," Trevor added.

"We'd like to see it and will be there in a minute," Norman began.

It was at that point that Trevor went back into the living room. "Should we worry about this Brock Ferguson man being on the loose?" asked Rhonda.

"No, unless he happens to come here, then I think it's safe to say that we don't have to be the least bit concerned," Margaret answered.

They then went into the living room to go see what Trevor had built with the Lego blocks. "What do you think?" inquired Trevor.

"It's very impressive, especially that you did it in such a short time," Norman replied.

"Thank you, sir. I really worked on it. I think that I'm going to make some other things, as well, because I have a few other ideas," Trevor said.

"You should get started on them right away, and after dinner, we can come back in and see what else you made," Margaret replied.

"That reminds me, you and I should start making dinner now," Birdie told her.

"What do you have that we can make?" asked Margaret.

"I saw a few things in the freezer but couldn't tell what they were. I think the best way for us to decide is to pull them all out. We also have a couple of side dishes, as well, that we haven't used yet," Rhonda answered.

They then left and went into the kitchen. Trevor continued to make different things out of the Lego blocks until he had a whole bunch of stuff. When it was finally time to eat dinner, Trevor was the first person to sit down because he smelled what was cooking from all the way inside the living room. "What is it that smells so good?" inquired Trevor.

"That's the tuna noodle casserole. It should be done in another very soon, like, in another two to three minutes," Margaret replied.

"What happened to cooking what we have in the freezer?" asked Norman.

"Well, everything was too frozen and would take a while to thaw out, so Margaret and I decided to make this instead. It's our mother's own recipe. We're also having green beans and roasted potatoes as side dishes," Birdie answered.

"Do you think the potatoes need to be cooked a little bit more?" inquired Margaret.

"No, they should be alright, but it's the green beans that I am more worried about because they have been cooking for a while now," Rhonda replied.

"I am keeping an eye on everything and am checking frequently, so there's no need to worry," Margaret began.

It was then that Trevor let out a big yawn. "Maybe you should go to bed right after dinner because you seem to be tired," Norman said.

"Yes, I am a little bit, sir, and I think I will go to bed once we have finished eating dinner, but I'll be fine until then," Trevor replied.

At that point, the food was ready, and both Margaret and Birdie put everything on the table. "Is everything good?" asked Margaret.

"Yes, you two did very well. The tuna noodle casserole is exceptional, as are the green beans, but I haven't tried the roasted potatoes yet," Norman answered.

"Do you want some more, Trevor?" inquired Rhonda.

"Yes, but just a small portion because I'm already kind of full but, at the same time, a little bit hungry," Trevor replied.

"What's for dessert?" asked Norman.

"We found a few different flavors of ice cream in the freezer and already put them out on the counter to defrost," Margaret answered.

After they ate dinner, Trevor went right upstairs to sleep, Norman checked the stock market on his computer in his office, and Margaret and Birdie sat together at the dining room table once they had cleaned up everything for dinner and were looking through their mother's old cookbook, which was in a drawer in one of the upstairs rooms.

Outside, standing across the street, was Brock Ferguson. He had reappeared and knew that he had to hold off for a little bit before he could make his move. Now that he had gone rogue, Mr. Ferguson was going to take matters into his own hands, but the waiting was making him even more unhinged than ever. It was becoming too much for Brock, and he had to use all his willpower to stop himself from launching his assault at that very moment. He then turned and strode off as fast as he could because Mr. Ferguson saw a patrolling police car that was approaching.

As for Margaret and Birdie, they had kept their promise to their uncle about keeping Trevor safe. What they were unaware of was that this was only the beginning of another scheme planned out by Brock. It was only a matter of time before he acted upon it, but until then, Mr. Ferguson went back into hiding again.

As Trevor slept, he had a feeling that someone who wanted to harm him was close by. Suddenly he awoke and got out of bed. Trevor went over to the window and looked out but didn't see anyone. Then he got back into bed and went back to sleep.

Trevor's feeling had been right because Mr. Ferguson had returned to where he was before and stood there for a few more minutes before taking off again for good. Whatever Brock's objective was, one thing was for certain: it was something atrocious. Despite that, there were much more important things going on because Trevor was going to discover something that he never knew and always had wondered about. He was in for the shock of his life.

Trevor had thought that he had finally seen the last of the villainous foes after he had been rescued by Norman and his two nieces. However, they weren't done just yet because Albert Swindle and the remaining members of his group were inclined to strive to do away with Trevor, especially Mr. Swindle and Spyder, who were at their wits' end with him and wanted to obtain the money from the will soon. But Mr. Ferguson was a step ahead of them, and when all the waiting was over, he'd be ready to strike.

CHAPTER 15

Illustrates Trevor Discovering the Truth about His Parents and the Circumstances behind What Really Happened on the Night of His Birth

It was the first hour of the day. Morning had arrived once again, and the birds were chirping in the trees. Those who heard it would instantly feel relaxed. The beginning of the day was serene and filled with gaiety, a merriment embraced by many who saw morning as a symbol of rejuvenation. No matter how anyone thought of it, one thing was certain: there wasn't anything better than opening your eyes after a long sleep to greet the new day. This practice is very useful and should always be kept in mind as a tool for everyday life, even though it's full of surprises and can be unpredictable.

Trevor was having a very strange dream, unlike the nightmares he used to have. This one was about his parents, although he never knew them. Trevor still dreamt about them occasionally, vividly seeing them as if they had not died at all. But he awoke suddenly, realizing it was morning. Trevor lay there, trying to comprehend his dream, but it didn't make much sense to him. Deciding not to go back to sleep, he quietly got out of bed and went downstairs. As he made his way down the stairs, Trevor almost reached the bottom before stopping. He knew Margaret and Rhonda might be up soon, then he continued down.

Without thinking, Trevor found his way into the room with the piano. There was also a small love seat, upon which he sat. Trevor couldn't stop thinking about his dream, no matter how hard he tried; it stayed in his head. An hour later, Margaret got up, followed by Birdie an hour after.

"What should we have for breakfast?" asked Rhonda.

"It depends on what we have. I know we're out of eggs and bacon, but we still have a few boxes of different cereals that aren't opened," Margaret answered.

"What kind are there?" inquired Trevor.

"Let us look, and we'll let you know. I think we bought a box of something that Trevor will like, and you and I can have one of the healthier ones," Birdie replied.

"Which one should I give Trevor?" asked Margaret.

"It's the yellow-and-blue box. The other ones we can choose what we like," Rhonda answered.

"You know, I was having the strangest dream. It was about my parents. I never really dreamt of them that much," Trevor began.

"Well, I know that they would have loved you a lot, especially your mother. She was a very kind, caring person," Margaret said.

"Trevor dear, you can tell us later about your dream. I'm sure it was something wonderful that we'd all like to hear," Birdie replied.

After they finished eating, Trevor played with a set of dominoes. He lined them up all around the living room and made them all topple down, which amused him in the early afternoon. Norman had awoken and gone downstairs, appearing as if he had something he wanted to tell them.

"Is there something wrong, Uncle?" inquired Rhonda.

"No, I was just thinking about something, that's all," Norman replied.

"Can you tell us what it is?" asked Margaret.

Norman then looked at Trevor. "Do you wish to know about your parents and how they died?" he inquired.

"Oh, yes, sir, I would very much so," Trevor answered.

"Alright then, let's go into the living room." They all went into the living room.

"Do you think this is a good idea to tell him now?" asked Margaret.

"Yes, I'm sure that Trevor has wondered his whole life about his parents, and I think that now is a good time to tell him about them," Norman replied.

"Where should you begin?" asked Margaret.

"I think from when Trevor's parents met each other for the very first time would be a good place to start," Birdie answered.

"Do you remember that portrait that was in the attic?" inquired Norman.

"Yes, sir, I do very much so. I haven't stopped wondering who that beautiful woman was," Trevor answered.

"She was your mother, Grace, who was also our uncle's younger sister and our aunt," Margaret began.

Trevor had a look of shock on his face. "So that would mean that you're my uncle? I never would have believed such a thing," he said.

"It's all true. Your parents met unexpectedly at a bar one night and later fell in love, but your father had a dark side to him that he hid from your mother at first," Norman replied.

"What do you mean by that, sir?" asked Trevor.

"To put it in a way you can understand, he liked to drink alcohol, and when he drank too much, he became very violent, which brings me to the night that you were born," replied Norman. "I seem to remember that about Uncle Malcolm. He refused to get help for it and just became worse over time," Birdie told them.

"What was his last name again?" inquired Margaret.

"It was Donner, but the night of Trevor's birth, Malcolm went out drinking for a few hours early that night but drank too much. When he got home, he and Grace had an argument over something, which caused Malcolm to become violent and caused physical harm to my sister, who was pregnant at the time," Norman answered.

"I seem to remember hearing that it was so bad that Grace fled the house and wandered around in the rain for some time and found a church to take refuge. That explains why Trevor was born in that exact church that was in the city of Boca Raton, if I can remember correctly," Rhonda began.

"How did she die?" asked Trevor.

"I was just going to get to that. The employees of the church found Grace all worn out. It was then that her water broke, and a little bit after, Trevor was born. Had I known that he was related to me, I might have gone and taken Trevor out of that dreaded church and raised him myself. I know that is a lot to take in, but please believe me when I say it's all true," Norman replied.

Trevor just sat there silently. He looked very surprised by all that he had just heard. "Uncle Malcolm's cause of death?" inquired Birdie. "They said that it was a heart attack brought on by ongoing smoking. He used to smoke a whole pack of cigarettes a day. That's something that was another addiction that he struggled with," Norman answered.

"What was my mother like?" asked Trevor.

"She was a very kind and caring person that I can remember. She was also very thoughtful. She used to come over for Christmas dinner every year when we were little. It makes me very sad that she passed away. I wish that there were more people in this world like her," Margaret replied.

"Yes, I agree with that. There's not a day that goes by that I don't miss Grace, but know that she's in a better place now and is no longer suffering or in any kind of pain," Norman said.

"If only Uncle Malcolm wouldn't have gotten help, then perhaps she would still be alive," Rhonda replied.

"The problem with Malcolm was that he didn't have the willpower to want to do that. He'd rather keep drinking than become sober," Norman told them.

"Do you really think that's true?" inquired Birdie.

"I do. If he truly loved Aunt Grace that much, then he would have stopped drinking. But because he chose not to, it's a sign of weakness," Margaret answered.

"Yes, that is the truth. His bad choices are what caused his own downfall. My sister was the victim in all of this. It might have been a good idea if she had just divorced him before things started to spiral out of control, then she would have been alright," Norman began.

"Why didn't she do that?" asked Margaret.

"It's probably because she was afraid that he might eventually come after her, so she had to endure all her suffering. That's why she coped with it," Rhonda replied.

"It does make me think that I should have stepped in and done something about it once I had found out what was going on. Now it's one of my biggest regrets," Norman said.

It was then that Trevor got up and left the room without saying anything.

"Where are you going, Trevor?" inquired Margaret.

"Just let him go. This is obviously a lot for him to process," Norman answered.

"Do you think we made a mistake by telling him now?" asked Birdie.

"No, it wasn't. He has a right to know the truth about his parents and what happened on the night of his birth," Margaret replied.

"What's for lunch today?" asked Norman.

"We haven't decided that yet, but I'm very concerned about Trevor because he seemed very upset, and it kind of makes me feel guilty about it," Rhonda answered.

"He'll be alright. It will just take a little time, but I know that he'll be back to his happy self again," Norman told them.

"Maybe we should get started on lunch. We still have to decide on what we're going to make," Margaret began. "I have an idea. Let's make something that Trevor really likes. That might help with cheering him up a bit," Birdie said.

"What does he like the most that you cook?" inquired Norman.

They then thought about it for a minute until Margaret spoke.

"I just thought of something. We can have grilled cheese sandwiches with tomato soup for the three of us," she replied.

"Do you think Trevor will like it?" asked Rhonda.

"Of course, he will. And then I'm positive that he'll forget all about the conversation that we had," Margaret answered.

It was then that they left the room and went into the kitchen to start making lunch. Trevor hadn't been seen since they had explained to him about his parents, and while Norman and Margaret weren't the least bit worried, Birdie, on the other hand, still was, and it caused her to be distracted while she was cooking lunch. But once it was ready, to their surprise, Trevor had gone down after being in his room. "What's that you're cooking?" he inquired.

"We're having grilled cheese sandwiches, but we're all having tomato soup with ours. Do us a favor, and go tell Uncle Norman that lunch is ready," Margaret replied.

Trevor then went to Norman's office. He knocked on the door and waited for a response. "Who is it?" asked Norman.

"It's Trevor, sir," Trevor answered.

"Come right in, my dear child," Norman answered.

So Trevor entered the office where Norman was busy doing something but stopped right away. "I just came to tell you that lunch is ready, sir," Trevor said.

"Thank you. I will be there very soon, but there is something that I want to tell you before we eat," Norman replied.

"What is it, sir?" inquired Trevor.

"I hope that you're still not that upset about what we told you. Just know that our intentions were good, and we felt that it was the right time to tell you," Norman replied.

"I am a little, sir, but I will be alright. I was just shocked to hear such a thing," Trevor began.

"That's good to hear. Now let's go eat because I'm very hungry, and I'm sure you must be, too," Norman said.

They then left the office together and went into the kitchen. "What took you two so long?" asked Rhonda.

"I was just having a little chat with Trevor to make sure that he's alright," Norman answered.

They sat down at the table, and a little after that, lunch was ready. "Are you sure you're alright?" inquired Margaret to Trevor.

"Oh yes, I was very sad at first after hearing about my parents, but I was even more so about how my mother had died and that my father was a very bad man," Trevor replied.

"He wasn't a bad man at all, but just made a lot of bad choices that turned him into a completely different person," Norman began.

"Why do you think he did all that stuff?" asked Birdie.

"He never told anyone the reason, but whatever it was, he should have realized all of the damage it was causing and did something about it," Norman answered.

"What should we do after lunch?" inquired Trevor. "I was thinking that we could all go out to see a movie because I haven't gone for a very long time," Margaret replied. "I wonder what's playing. One of us should look, and we can decide together which one to see," Rhonda said.

"Do you still have today's newspaper?" asked Margaret.

"Yes, I will look after lunch in there and see if there is an age-appropriate movie that we can go see," Norman answered.

After lunch, Norman went back into his office and looked in the newspaper. He found a movie that was rated G and started in an hour, and he told the others. When it was time to go, they got into Norman's car, which was parked in the driveway. While they were about to leave, Trevor thought he saw someone who resembled Brock Ferguson standing across the street from them. He stopped in his tracks and froze.

"What's the matter, Trevor?" inquired Birdie.

"For a second, I thought I saw that homeless man who helped kidnap me. He's standing over there," Trevor replied.

"There's no one there. Your eyes must be playing tricks on you. He doesn't know where we live. You don't have to fear anything," Norman told him.

They then left for the local multiplex theater. Trevor had a small bag of popcorn with a little bit of butter on it. He really enjoyed the movie, and after it was over, they went a few doors down to an ice-cream shop where Trevor had a small cone of vanilla ice cream. Then they went back home.

As they were going into the house, Trevor looked back to see if the man who looked like Mr. Ferguson was still standing across the street again, but he saw no one and went into the house with the others. But what Trevor wasn't seeing things—Brock had come back after vanishing for a few days and was lurking nearby their house again. However, Mr. Ferguson was trying his best to not be seen by anyone.

Trevor spent the remainder of the afternoon in his room, creating and playing a game with a bag of toy soldiers, which were on a shelf in Norman's office. Once Trevor had gotten tired of doing that, he found a notebook that had blank pages. He didn't know whom it belonged to but asked permission before writing anything in it.

Trevor started writing a short story, and by the time dinner was ready, he had already written eight pages and decided to finish it after dinner. When Trevor got there, he sat right down at the table where Norman had just sat down. Margaret and Rhonda were just about done cooking, and when everything was done, they put it out on the table.

"What did you use that notebook for?" asked Margaret.

"I started writing a fictional short story but haven't finished it yet," Trevor answered.

"That's great! Once you get done with it, would you read it to us?" Norman suggested.

"What's it about?" inquired Birdie.

"It's sort of hard to explain, but I will try my best. The plot is about a faraway land, and this prince goes on a long journey to rescue a princess from an evil sorceress who kidnapped her," Trevor replied.

"That sounds so interesting. I'm really looking forward to hearing the entire story," Margaret said.

"Have you thought of an ending for your story?" asked Norman.

"No, I'm still trying to think of one. It's like no matter how hard I try, nothing comes to mind," Trevor answered.

"It will come to you, maybe when you least expect it to," Rhonda told him.

When they had finished eating dinner, Trevor went back upstairs to his room to write some more of his story. He worked on seven more pages before he brushed his teeth, put on his pajamas, and went to sleep. But as Trevor slept, he was not aware of the fact that Brock was now standing in their front yard. Brock looked up at the window of Trevor's room, gripping his shillelagh tightly in his right hand, then went on his way again.

Now that Trevor knew the truth about his parents and what had occurred on the night that he was born, he was still trying to process it. But he was no longer sad about it. Even though it came as a surprise to Trevor, he was somewhat glad that he now knew something about his parents. However, Trevor wanted to find out a lot more and thought about asking Norman, but he thought that it might not be such a good idea.

What Trevor didn't know was that what was about to happen next would be something that was going to bring closure to some of his troubles. However, there was still more to it because Spyder and Albert Swindle had yet to be caught and taken into custody by the police. This was because they had a hard time tracking them down. Additionally, they discovered that it was, in fact, Mr. Ferguson who was the one who had killed Abigail. Soon, everything would be revealed, as the final showdown was about to begin.

CHAPTER 16

The Final Showdown

The church bell rang out, signaling Sunday morning. While most people were preparing to attend a service, for some, Sundays were more about relaxation and enjoying the last day of the weekend. The ritual of leisure was often deemed more pleasurable than sitting through an entire church service every week. However, for others, attending church was about being a good Christian and maintaining faith.

This diversity in perspectives is evident in various aspects of life. Ultimately, it is up to each individual to determine their beliefs and how they perceive religion. Some may seek closeness to God, while others focus on making small improvements in their lives to cultivate their own indomitable spirit, thus inspiring and motivating others.

Meanwhile, Trevor remained asleep, having turned over only once during the night. As the sunlight streamed through his window, it stirred him awake. Rubbing his eyes and stretching his arms, Trevor realized it wasn't too early. Retrieving his notebook, he resumed work on his short story. Almost finished, he had penned the perfect ending before falling asleep, ensuring he wouldn't forget it.

While engrossed in his writing, Trevor heard footsteps approaching his room. Panic set in as he wondered who it might be, hoping it wasn't Brock. Hastily, he scrambled back into bed, hiding under the covers. The footsteps drew nearer until the doorknob turned, and someone entered the room. Trembling with fear, Trevor felt his heart race as the figure approached his bed, leaving him crouched and on edge, ready to scream.

"What are you doing?" asked a soothing voice. Trevor then took the covers off him to see that it was only Margaret. "I thought that you were that homeless man and were going to kill me," Trevor answered.

"I understand that you're still afraid after what had happened, but just know that it won't ever again because those bad people will never be able to come anywhere near you as long as we are in our home. You can always feel safe with us around," Margaret began.

"Is Rhonda awake yet?" inquired Trevor. "I think she is. I went by her room and heard something stirring in it. Let's head downstairs, and Birdie should be down shortly," Margaret replied.

They then went downstairs to the kitchen. A little bit after they had gotten there, they were joined by Rhonda. "Should we have breakfast now?" she asked.

"Yes, I would like an omelet, but only if you can make it," Trevor answered.

"Yes, we can. That's one of the first things our mother taught us to make when we started learning how to cook," Birdie said. "I remember that we made omelets quite a few times before being able to do it without any help," Margaret replied.

"What do you want in it?" inquired Rhonda.

"I'm not really sure because I didn't know that you can put things in omelets," Trevor told them.

"Do you like American cheese and ham?" inquired Margaret.

"I don't think that I've had either one before, but I wouldn't mind trying it," Trevor replied.

"I feel like having the same thing as Trevor but putting only tomatoes in mine and maybe a little bit of bell peppers," Birdie added.

"What are those?" asked Trevor.

"They're something that I don't think that you would like. I tend to gravitate more towards the orange and yellow ones because they're sweeter tasting," Rhonda answered.

"What are you going to have?" inquired Trevor.

"I think I'm going to have a blueberry muffin because that always seems to fill me right up," Margaret replied.

Once Trevor's omelet was ready, he ate only half of it, partly because it was big, but despite that, he really enjoyed it. After breakfast, Trevor decided that he would finish his story before he went to sleep. He went into the garage to see what hadn't been cleaned out yet and discovered in a big plastic container some old comics, which inspired him to create his own. He knew that before he could do that, he had to finish his short story first. Trevor had a lot more ideas and wrote them all down.

In the early afternoon, Norman woke up. Before going downstairs to his office, he went into Trevor's room, where Trevor was scanning through the pages and panels of the comics. "Oh, hello there, sir. I was looking at these old comics," Trevor told him.

"Where did you find those?" asked Norman.

"They were in a big plastic container that was in the garage. There were so many of them that I only took a few and left the rest," Trevor answered.

"It must have been hidden behind when you were helping Margaret and Birdie clean out the garage. Since you found them, they are yours to keep because I don't have any desire to read them. If you need help getting the others from the garage, I can bring them up here to your room," Norman said.

"I would very much appreciate that, sir, because I am going to try to make my own," Trevor replied.

"I'm so happy to hear that you're using your time to be so creative. Perhaps one day you can become a famous artist or a writer, maybe both if you really work at it. I'm going to go downstairs now, but you keep up all of the good work. I can't wait to see what else you create," Norman told him.

He then left to go downstairs to his office. But before doing that, Norman headed to the garage to get the rest of the comics. Once he did that, Norman headed back upstairs. On the way, he was stopped by Margaret. "What are you doing with those?" she inquired.

"Trevor found them in the garage, but there was too much for him to take all of them. So he only took a few. I'm bringing him the rest now before I do my stuff in my office," Norman replied.

"What do you want for lunch?" asked Margaret.

"That all depends on what Rhonda and you want to make. It's fine with me, but I want to bring these up to Trevor because this container is very heavy," Norman answered. He then went upstairs to give the rest of the comics to Trevor.

When he got there, Trevor was still going through the stack of comics. "Where do you want me to put these?" inquired Norman.

"I was thinking in that little corner by my desk because it would make it easier for me to get to them," Trevor replied. So Norman put the container of comics down where Trevor wanted them. Norman was going to go back downstairs to his office but was stopped suddenly because Trevor spoke.

"Can you tell me more about my mother, sir?" he asked.

"Later, I will set aside some time to do that. There's a lot more that I want to tell you, but I don't have the time to do it now. We can do it after dinner because I'll be free then," Norman answered.

"Yes, let's do it then. I would like to hear all about her before I go to sleep. I once had a dream about her, or at least I think it was," Trevor added.

Norman then left to go back downstairs. A little bit afterward, lunch was ready. After that, Trevor used the rest of the time to scan through the comics some more. But because there were so many, he had to do it slowly. Once Trevor finished one, he put it to the side and went to the next. This took up a lot of his time that lasted until dinner. Once they had finished, Trevor was going to go back to his room, but Norman caused him to halt abruptly and almost lose his balance and fall.

"Don't you want me to tell you more about your mother?" he inquired.

"Yes, but I want to finish up my short story. So if we can postpone it until tomorrow when you have some free time," Trevor replied. He then went up to his room to write the rest of his short story. While he was doing that, Trevor yawned a few times and realized that he was starting to get very tired. He was in the middle of writing a sentence. After he finished it, he got changed, brushed his teeth, and went to sleep. Time slipped by because soon it was already midnight. During his sleep, Trevor was awakened suddenly after hearing a noise downstairs and went to see what it was.

He crept down the stairs as quietly as he could. When Trevor had gotten halfway, he saw a stray cat on the windowsill. The cat was meowing very loudly. Trevor motioned to it to stop and go away, but the cat just kept on meowing. Eventually, it got tired of sitting on the windowsill and jumped off. Once Trevor had gotten downstairs, it was completely dark. He looked around but didn't see anyone.

Just then, Brock Ferguson came up from behind him and put his hand over Trevor's mouth, then he picked up Trevor and stuffed him into a potato sack. Brock then exited out of the window he had come in through. Mr. Ferguson moved very fast to wherever he was going. Trevor fidgeted and yelled to be let out, but Mr. Ferguson just kept going without acknowledging him. At one point, Trevor heard Brock going up the steps and knocking on a door, as well as a voice saying, "What another glorious night." Trevor could also smell cigar smoke from inside the sack.

"Why, Brock, I didn't expect to see you here anytime soon," Albert Swindle said. "I need to speak with you right away, it's very important," Mr. Ferguson began. "Is everything alright?" asked Mr. Swindle. "If you let me come in, I will explain to you what's going on," Brock answered. "Come in, we have a lot to catch up on. But first, you can tell me what you need to tell me," Albert Swindle said.

"Don't be so cordial, Swindle. There are things that I'm going to tell you that you wouldn't believe," Mr. Ferguson replied. Then Brock entered the caravan and saw Mr. Swindle's pupils all rushing around, taking heads off the walls and putting things into sacks.

"What the hell is going on?" inquired Brock. "We're relocating. The cops know where we are, and they'll be here any minute now, so we can't stay around for too much longer," Mr. Swindle replied. "I'm afraid that we have bigger problems to worry about, Swindle. The jig may be up for you, but I'm not giving up," Mr. Ferguson told him.

"What do you mean by that?" asked Albert Swindle. "There's something that you should know, but I can't say it in front of these little brats. So let's go into your room so we can talk privately," Brock answered. It was then that Trevor fidgeted some more and yelled to be let out of the sack.

"What do you have in there?" inquired Mr. Swindle. "If we can go into your room, I will gladly show you. I think you'll like it a lot," Mr. Ferguson replied. So they went into Albert Swindle's room and shut the door. But what they didn't know was that Nathan had stopped what he was doing and strode over to the door of Mr. Swindle's room, listening to the conversation.

"Get away from there before you get us all in trouble with Swindle," snapped Robert Porter. "No, I think I know what they're talking about. And if I'm right, then we could turn Swindle into the police when they arrive," Nathan began. He continued to listen until he heard Albert Swindle and Brock going toward the door, then quickly ran away from the door to help the others pack.

It was at that point that Mr. Swindle and Mr. Ferguson went out of the room. "What should I do with this, sir?" asked Mrs. Porter. "Put it over there in that sack because most of the others are already full. It seems she's not as bright as I thought. You should have taught her better, Mr. Porter," Albert Swindle answered. Robert Porter didn't say anything and just made an angry face, then he continued putting more stuff into one of the sacks until it was full.

"Where are you going to go?" inquired Brock. "I haven't really thought much about it, but it has to be somewhere far away where the police can never find me," Mr. Swindle replied. "If I were you, I would start thinking otherwise. You'll never make it to safety in time. The cops might be here sooner than you think," Mr. Ferguson said.

"I know that, but my pupils can't work any faster. They are going at their own pace. Even when I shout at them to go faster, they still don't listen, even though they know that we have to evacuate as soon as possible," Albert Swindle replied.

"Are you saying that you're just going to leave your caravan here?" asked Brock.

"There's nothing else that I can do. If I take it with me, then eventually the police will be able to track it and me down. That's why I have to abandon it. It makes me very sad, but I have no other choice," Mr. Swindle answered.

"Well, I wish you the best of luck wherever you go. It's been nice knowing and working alongside you, but I better get going now. If the cops know I'm here, we will both be in the dog house," Mr. Ferguson told him.

It was then that Albert Swindle was about to say something, but suddenly he stopped and was quiet. "Do you hear that?" he inquired.

"Yes, it's the sound of sirens. That must mean the police are nearby, and it's now time for me to make my exit. Farewell to you," Brock added.

He was about to go, but after seeing lights from sirens, he stopped in his tracks, and they heard a policeman's voice. "Albert Swindle, we have your caravan surrounded. Come out with your hands up. If you don't come quietly, we will be forced to enter."

"What should we do, sir?" asked Nathan.

"I have an idea. Everyone, go out the window that's in the second room. Nathan, I'm putting you in charge of leading the others. Now hurry up and go," Mr. Swindle replied.

"What about you?" inquired Mrs. Porter.

"Don't worry about me. I'll be just fine. You just worry about yourself. Go, all of you, no arguments. Get going quickly now," Albert Swindle answered.

It was at that point that Mr. Swindle's pupils all followed Nathan to the second room and went out the window one by one. "What should we do now?" asked Brock.

"I think it would be smart if you went out the back window, as well. It's big enough that you can fit through it," Albert Swindle replied.

"Brilliant idea, Swindle. If you're going to sacrifice yourself for the rest of us, then I will gladly go if it means not getting caught. Goodbye," Mr. Ferguson began. He then hurried toward the second room and went out the window.

With the others safely out of harm's way, Mr. Swindle knew what he had to do. "This is your last chance, Swindle. Come out, or we'll come in there," the voice of the same policeman shouted.

Albert Swindle drew a big breath and started toward the door of his caravan. What he was unaware of was that the cigar that he had been smoking earlier was on the armrest of the couch and that the fire from it had spread onto his clothes, but he hadn't noticed it yet.

When Albert Swindle had gone out, there was a crowd of angry people all around. The cops came up and arrested Mr. Swindle. While they were taking him to the police car, the crowd of angry people yelled, cursed, and threw stuff at Albert Swindle. One person went as far as to get close enough to spit on him. He saw in the crowd Robert Porter, who just looked at him in disbelief and shook his head.

Before Swindle was put into the back of the police car, a man stepped forward. "Does anyone else smell smoke?" he inquired. Everyone looked around only to see that Mr. Swindle's right arm was on fire. He jumped around, yelling, "Someone help me! I'm on fire!"

"What should we do?" asked one of the policemen. "There's a river nearby. Here, go fill this cup up with the water from it, and make it quick before the fire spreads to the rest of his body," the same policeman who had been shouting for Albert Swindle to come out said. He then poured out the coffee that had been in the cup and handed it to the other policeman, who ran to the river to get the water. Mr. Swindle continued to jump around and yell for someone to help him. It didn't take the other policeman too long to return; he splashed the water onto Albert Swindle's arm, putting out the fire but leaving very bad burns. It was then that Mr. Swindle was taken away by the police. The crowd of people then disbanded, leaving the caravan where it was.

Brock walked as fast as he could to get away. He managed to end up at an abandoned building. He went up the steps and knocked on the door, "Who's there?" asked a voice. "Open up, you dunderheads!" Mr. Ferguson answered. He could hear more voices talking. "I think it might be Spyder." The door opened, and Brock went in to see that Bishop, Zeke, and Doc were in there. "Sorry, Mr. Ferguson, we had to make sure that it wasn't the police because for some reason, they've been around here all day," Doc told them. "Barricade the door again, Zeke. No one else is to come in," Bishop began. "Yes, sir. You don't have to worry about a thing. It will be done," the African American bartender said, and he laid two big pieces of wooden boards across the door. "How did you know we were here?" inquired Bishop. "It was Swindle who told me. I tried to get here without being seen, which wasn't that easy, let me tell you, but I did it," Brock replied.

"What's the news regarding Albert Swindle?" asked Zeke. "It's not good. That's about all that I can tell you, but from here on out, it's every person for themselves," Mr. Ferguson answered. "It looks like we're all that's left and that this is the end," Doc added. "Yes, I'm sad to say that it is, my friend. We had everything going for us, and I can't seem to think what went wrong," Bishop began, shaking his head. "All hope isn't lost. Spyder is still somewhere out there. He might be our only hope. We have to think that he hasn't thrown in the towel just yet," Mr. Ferguson said. "Yes, but if that is true, then it's all up to him now. With Swindle out of the picture, we have no one else left to rely on," Bishop replied. It was then that they heard a noise outside. Brock hurried towards the window to see that another crowd of angry people and the police were standing below them. "Who's out there?" asked Zeke. "No one, just some drunk people who are passing by," Mr. Ferguson replied. "It's over, Brock. You might as well just come quietly and make it easier on yourself. We know that it was you who killed that Abigail girl," a policeman yelled loudly. The others looked like they had seen a ghost. "Did you really kill her?" inquired Doc.

"Yes, but she had betrayed us, so I did it for all of us," Brock answered.

"How could you do such a thing?" inquired Bishop. "Oh, come on, don't act like you wouldn't have done the same thing if you had to. It's her fault that we're in this whole mess, Doc. You know me, right?" Mr. Ferguson replied.

"Don't come anywhere near me, horrible monster! We looked up to you as a trusted leader, and you go and do a thing like this," Doc told him. He then went to run over to the door, took the two boards off it, and ran down to the crowd of people. Brock tried to stop him, but Doc was too fast for him. They could hear the police going toward them. Mr. Ferguson then started to climb out of the window, but the police had already arrived, led by Doc.

"Give yourself up, Ferguson. Swindle has been captured. It's all over," another policeman began.

"No, I am going down, and then you all are going with me, even if I have to kill every single one of you myself!" Brock shouted. He then climbed out of the window and shimmied up a nearby drainpipe onto the roof of the building. He still had Trevor in the sack. The police pulled out their guns and began shooting at Mr. Ferguson, but they weren't able to get him.

Among the many people in the crowd were Norman, Margaret, and Rhonda. "Isn't there anything that we can do?" asked Birdie.

"No, we just have to let the police handle it," Norman answered. "There's no place left for you to go, Ferguson. I'll give you one last chance to give yourself up. If you refuse, then we'll have to come up there and bring you down ourselves," the same policeman who had been yelling before said.

"I'll never do that as long as I am still breathing. It will take more than just a few cops to stop me. You can try if you want, but it won't do you any good. You'll never take me alive!" Brock yelled. He started to climb higher up onto another part of the roof, but suddenly there was a gunshot, and Mr. Ferguson was shot in the head. He dropped the sack with Trevor in it and then fell off the roof and onto the ground. A few of the people stood around him, but the police intervened.

"Everyone stay back! I want this area to be completely clear. No one is to go anywhere near the body unless they're authorized to," another policeman began.

"What about Trevor?" inquired Margaret.

"They'll get him down from there somehow. I'm just glad that Ferguson is dead, and now that should be the last of Albert Swindle's group of villains," Norman replied.

"The children who were employed by him need to be found because they could testify against Swindle in his trial, which he'd be locked up for good," Birdie said.

"Even if the police were able to do that, they might still be loyal to him and wouldn't want to betray him," Margaret replied.

"Do you suppose they would?" inquired Rhonda.

"It's very likely. Only that boy up there was the only one who turned his back on his associates. The rest must have feared being persecuted and went into hiding somewhere," Norman answered.

It was then that the crowd of people all left, except for Norman, Margaret, and Birdie. The fire department arrived and rescued Trevor from the roof then took him over to where Norman, Margaret, and Rhonda were standing.

"Does this boy belong to you?" one of the firefighters asked.

"Yes, sir, he does. Thank you for rescuing him. We were worried that he might have fallen off because that roof doesn't look too sturdy," Margaret replied.

The fireman nodded and went on his way.

"We're so glad that you're alright. You had us worried there for a while," Birdie told him.

"I thought you would never find me. Everything happened so fast and made me very afraid," Trevor added.

"The truth is, at first, we didn't know where you went, but we were determined to get to the bottom of your disappearance. It took some time, but once we knew, we wasted no time in going to where you were," Margaret began.

"How did you find that out?" inquired Trevor.

"It wasn't so easy. We had to use some different resources this time, but it proved to have worked. And now that you're safe, we can go back to living our peaceful lives," Rhonda answered.

It was then that Trevor hugged all three of them. He had a big smile on his face, but when Trevor saw Brock lying there dead, the smile faded. He went over to the body and stood over it. The others soon joined him.

"That man was pure evil, and he finally got what he deserved. I wish that he could have seen the error of his ways sooner," Norman said.

"We shouldn't mourn his death nor show any pity towards him, because he chose to be the way he was and all that he did. People like him aren't deserving of such things," Margaret replied.

"Do you think he would have turned over a new leaf?" asked Birdie.

"I doubt it. He clearly wasn't anyone who seemed to have any good in him, and that's why, in the end, he got what was coming to him. Those who are wicked possess no remorse, empathy, or compassion.

They can't ever mend their ways. It's just a fact of life. They have no redeeming qualities in them," Norman answered.

"Why do you think he was like that?" inquired Margaret.

"Who knows, but for whatever reasons, they probably weren't good ones. Now, let's go home because it's already late, and we all need to get some sleep," Norman replied.

It was at that point that they left to go home. Mr. Ferguson was dead, and the others were nowhere to be found, except both Bishop and Doc, who left the scene shortly after Brock had been shot to death. The only one left was Albert Swindle, but he was in jail and awaiting trial. Just the thought of the villainous magician sitting in his cold, dark cell awaiting his fate seemed very eerie. However, Mr. Swindle was now deemed as a criminal and, because he had sacrificed himself, hoped that the judge would be lenient on him, although he had committed many crimes. The anticipation made Albert Swindle very anxious, and he was seen biting his fingernails and leaving the nails all over the ground of his cell.

Even though Mr. Swindle's group of villains had disbanded for good, Spyder had yet to be captured. His current whereabouts were unknown, and the police had turned their focus on finding him because he was the last person of Albert Swindle's group who needed to be found. There were still a few more things that had to be done before they could put to rest this whole thing about finding out Trevor's true identity, as well as never having to worry about any more bad people ever trying to go after Trevor.

What was going to happen next would be a big turning point, in which Trevor would return to where this all began and again come face-to-face with two more people from his past. Without Trevor even knowing it, it would surprisingly work out in his favor. Even though Trevor's mother's wedding ring was lying at the bottom of Biscayne Bay, Norman was able to uncover Trevor's true identity without it. Despite Spyder having no knowledge of this, he would soon find that all his efforts were in vain. When it all finally said and done, Trevor had gotten the better of those who had done him wrong throughout his life.

CHAPTER 17

Trevor Returns to His Place of Birth and Gets Retribution for How He Was Treated

Following the events of the previous night and because they were up almost until daylight, Trevor had slept in until the late afternoon. He tried to forget about what had happened; however, even though he knew that Brock Ferguson was dead and that no one could ever harm him again, Trevor felt very relieved because he never wanted to be involved with any more bad people. Trevor realized the difference between those who were good and those who weren't, something he had not known before.

Trevor woke up at around two thirty. He got right out of bed, changed his clothes, and then went downstairs to the kitchen. To his surprise, Norman and his two nieces were in there. "Good morning to you, Trevor. I hope that you slept well. I know I did," Margaret began. "She and Birde were making breakfast for us."

"Yes, I did and think that I have completely recovered from last night," Trevor said. "I think it's safe to say that no harm shall come to you now that Ferguson is gone and that Swindle's group of villains has disbanded permanently. There's no one else left that I can think of," Rhonda replied.

"What about that man Spyder asked?" Margaret questioned. "He was just lucky to have not been around when Swindle had been captured or where we were last night, or he might have been taken in too. But let's just hope that the police find him, then there really won't be anything left to worry about," Birde answered.

"Is breakfast almost ready?" inquired Norman. "Yes, Uncle, it will be very soon. We're just about finished," Margaret replied. "What's the rush, sir?" asked Trevor. "We have a very important appointment that is in a city south of here. It will take us a while to get there, so we should get on our way as soon as possible," Norman answered.

"That's funny. I don't remember you mentioning anything about an appointment today. You usually tell us these things ahead of time," Rhonda told him. "I meant to but just completely forgot. But we must leave on time in order to arrive promptly at our destination," Norman began.

"Where exactly is it?" inquired Margaret. "You will just have to wait and see. I looked it up on a map and was able to find the street where it's located," Norman replied. "Breakfast is ready, everyone. We're going to bring it over to the table right now. I hope you two are hungry," Birde said, and she and Margaret then brought their breakfast and placed it on the table.

After they finished eating, they got into the car and drove down south to Boca Raton. "Why does this look familiar to me?" inquired Trevor. "It's because we're in your birth city and partially raised," Margaret answered. They then turned a corner, and there was the church where Trevor had been born. When he saw it, he was filled with fear but kept it inside.

Once they parked, they walked toward the entrance, but Trevor stopped suddenly. "What's the matter, Trevor?" asked Rhonda. "I can't go in there, not after all the bad memories I have. I thought I would never have to see this place ever again," Trevor replied. "You have nothing to fear, my dear child. When you first came here, you hadn't anyone who cared about you. Now you're returning with people who do, and you don't have to worry about anything. Trust us," Norman told him.

They all walked together and went into the front office to check in with the receptionist. Then they walked past a few classrooms. One of them Trevor recognized as the one he had been in. That brought back a lot of bad memories for him. They went into the chapel and sat down to wait. It was then that one of the employees went in. "Should I tell them you're ready for them now?" he asked. "Yes, have them come in," Norman answered. He then went back out into the hallway, and at that moment, Pastor Swanson and his wife entered.

"Do my eyes deceive me? Why, it's little Trevor! We have been worried sick about you and wondered where you had gone," Pastor Swanson began. "That's enough out of you. We're here on Trevor's behalf because we got word that you two were in cahoots with a man named Spyder," Norman said. "I wasn't. It was all him. I didn't have a hand in any of this. I swear to you, if you are to persecute anyone, it should only be him," Mrs. Swanson replied.

"You can't lie your way out of this. There is evidence against both of you that you met with Spyder and accepted a bribe of money from him in exchange for information about Trevor. You also gave him a wedding ring that belonged to Trevor's mother," Margaret told them.

"How dare you accuse us of such things! We are good Christians who go by what the Good Book says and would never do anything so sinful," Mrs. Swanson added.

"What do you know about it?" inquired Pastor Swanson. "The police were onto you from the beginning. They had done a background check on both of you, and it was confirmed what you did," Rhonda replied. "That's impossible! There's no way that the police could have known unless they were following us," Mrs. Swanson began.

"You are correct about that. The police did, in fact, follow you when you met with Spyder that night down in Miami. They know that he threw the ring into the bay because he believed that by doing that, we wouldn't be able to discover Trevor's true identity," Norman said.

"Look here, sir. I am a very patient man, but I will not tolerate your outrageous accusations against us," Pastor Swanson replied angrily as he stood up. "Are you two willing to sign a confession about all the things you did?" inquired Rhonda. "No, we will do no such thing because what you people say isn't true. I know it, and so does my husband. We have a clean conscience," Mrs. Swanson answered.

"Perhaps then we should get the police who had followed you, and they can prove that you did," Margaret told them.

"There's no need to do that. We will both sign the confession stating everything that we did, right, dear?" Pastor Swanson added.

"Why should we give in to these people?" asked Mrs. Swanson.

"Because no matter what we say to try to get off the hook, it clearly won't work. They claim to have proof," Pastor Swanson replied.

"Are you going to sign the confession or not?" inquired Birdie.

"Alright, we'll do it, but only because we don't want any trouble from you people after this. We get paid very little to work here but don't really mind it," Mrs. Swanson answered.

Norman then pulled out a piece of paper and a pen and handed it to them. They both signed the confession then handed it back to Norman.

"Can we go now?" asked Pastor Swanson.

"Yes, you may. We're finished here and with the two of you," Norman answered.

They then got up and were about to leave, but Pastor Swanson turned back around. "One more thing. I hope that all of this won't affect our jobs here at the church," he began.

"As a matter of fact, it will. Because of what you did, I will see to it that you two are never in a position of power ever again," Norman told them.

"You can't do that. We're poor and have to find other ways to make money," Pastor Swanson said.

"You have abused the children of this church for way too long, and that includes Trevor, as well," Margaret replied.

"I would like to point out that I was the one who gave him his name, something that no one else might have done," Pastor Swanson replied.

"That doesn't matter. You should have thought about doing the right thing from the start. But because you didn't, you are now finally getting what's coming to you, and we will make sure that this church's reputation is ruined for good so that people know what bad people work here. Now get out of our sight," Rhonda told them.

They then left and argued with each other.

"Should we go home now?" asked Margaret.

"Yes, but there is one more stop we have to make. However, we did what we came here to do, and now that it's over, this place will no longer abuse innocent children," Norman replied.

They got up and left the chapel. They went out where Trevor's parents were buried. Trevor shed tears for both of them but mostly for his mother. On the way home, Trevor was silent, but the others still talked about what had occurred in the church.

"I think we should have them both arrested for all the bad things they did," Margaret said.

"As much as we would like to see that happen, the punishment should always fit the crime, and whatever happens to them should be good enough to make them learn their lesson," Norman replied.

"What do you think that will be?" inquired Birdie.

"I suppose it will be something horrible, and they will very much deserve it. That much, because like the saying goes, 'What goes around comes around.' That's something that people like them learn," Margaret answered.

"Why wouldn't you tell us where we were going?" asked Trevor.

"I didn't want you to have any anxiety about the fact that you were returning to the place where you were born. I know that it must have brought up a lot of painful memories for you. But now you can just think of it as a time from your past that can no longer haunt you," Norman replied.

"That's right, you have us now. We decided to adopt you so that you always have a home," Margaret told him.

"That's very kind of you all. I thought that I was only staying with you temporarily until I found some place else to live," Trevor began.

"Did you think that we were going to throw you out?" asked Rhonda.

"I would hope not, especially after you've been so good to me. I never want to have to wander the streets again," Trevor replied.

"You'll never have to and will always have a home with us. We never told you this before, but Birdie and I think of you as a little brother and our uncle as a son. You're a part of our family now, and we wouldn't have it any other way," Margaret told him.

When they got home, Trevor couldn't stop smiling. He went straight upstairs to his room, where he pulled out a picture of his parents and lay on his bed looking at it. After a few minutes, he put it away and reflected on the day's events. A little bit afterward, Margaret and Rhonda announced that dinner was ready.

"Sir, I recall that earlier you mentioned to us that Mr. Swindle had already been captured," Trevor added.

"Yes, that's what I saw on the news a few days ago. Apparently, he's being charged for other things like the murder of his rival and fellow magician, Woodrow Wiggins. The trial already took place, and he was found guilty and is currently waiting to receive the death penalty sometime this week," Norman began.

"Why didn't we know about that?" inquired Margaret.

"I'm surprised that you didn't. It's been all over the local news. I've been following it since they first aired the story," Norman answered.

"Did they say where he was being held?" asked Rhonda.

"Yes, at a maximum-security prison that is near the fairgrounds. Some of his former pupils came forward and testified against him, but it didn't say whether or not they were persecuted, as well," Norman replied.

"I wonder which one of them it was. To me, they're all guilty and shouldn't be given the least bit of sympathy," Margaret said.

"I would agree. However, the one who testified against Swindle did the right thing in my opinion. It was what else was needed to be able to seal his fate," Birdie replied.

"Did the news give the name of which one it is?" asked Trevor.

"It was that boy Nathan. He was found walking on the side of a dirt road late at night, but someone who was driving by saw him and picked him up. He told the person everything," Norman answered.

"What about the other two?" inquired Margaret.

"They have not been found yet, but I heard that the police are still trying to find them. The last time they were seen was during Swindle's capture," Rhonda replied.

"How could that be?" asked Norman.

"Someone saw three children escaping from the back of Swindle's caravan. They didn't see where it was that they were going because it was dark and they disappeared so quickly. That person also saw Ferguson do the same a little bit after them," Margaret replied.

"Why didn't they tell the police right away?" inquired Birdie.

"It must be because there were a lot of people and it was nearly impossible to get through such a big crowd," Norman answered.

"How did they know where Mr. Swindle was?" asked Trevor.

"I believe that the word spread all around and people wanted to be present for it, which I really don't understand at all," Margaret replied.

"I don't either. I would think that people would have better and more important things to do than gather to watch a bad man get arrested. It seems like such a waste of time," Rhonda told them.

"Where was Swindle when they found him?" inquired Margaret.

"Surprisingly, he was at a public campground but was the only one there at the time. That's where Ferguson had taken Trevor after he had broken into our house. Because the police found fingerprints on the doorknob of the front door that they confirmed belonged to Ferguson, it made it easier to keep track of where he was going," Norman answered.

Now that Trevor had gotten retribution on Pastor Swanson and his wife, even though it required him to return to his birthplace, it gave him a sense of pleasure knowing that their contentious abuse and neglect toward him had finally been justified. He also realized that he wouldn't have to ever worry about being in that kind of situation again; it was now just a memory of the horrible life that he had once lived. But when Trevor looked back, he realized that he had really grown up a lot since those days when he was being oppressed by the church employees.

One thing that Trevor didn't expect at all was to go see where his parents were buried, something that neither Pastor Swanson nor his wife had ever taken him to see. But because he didn't know them other than what Norman had told him, Trevor felt more sad for his mother, and a part of him wished that she were still alive because he wondered what it would have been like to have known her. Perhaps if Trevor had been born sooner, she could have taken him with her far away from his father. Although he remembered something that Norman had said about that Trevor's father wasn't always a bad man, it made him think about what drove him to change his ways, for it was something that he was having a tough time comprehending.

Now that Albert Swindle had been sentenced for his many atrocities and Brock Ferguson not able to terrorize anyone ever again, there was only one more person left who needed to be apprehended, and that was Spyder. But he hadn't been seen since before the villainous group had disbanded. Now it was time for Norman to devote all his time to track down where Spyder was and have him taken into custody for questioning.

The only thing that wasn't known to the police was his real name. However, Norman did further research and discovered that the villain who called himself Spyder was somehow linked to Trevor. After finding this out, Norman knew that he was the person who had to have Spyder arrested and put away for good and didn't want to put all the burden on his nieces.

Since they had gotten back from Boca Raton, the police had already started to search all over the area for Spyder. It was somewhere in the early evening, and there were several reports of sightings by a few locals who thought they saw men they thought were Spyder. But the police were too late getting to the locations. Out of his fondness for Trevor, no matter how long it took to find the real Spyder, neither Norman nor the police was going to let him get off scot-free. They were going to buckle down until Spyder was finally caught. Then it would be all over, and at long last, they'd be out of the woods because soon, everything would draw to a close, and Trevor would be safe and sound.

CHAPTER 18

Albert Swindle's Last Day Alive

It was a dreary morning; the sky was overcast, as it usually was, and the clouds were a dark gray color. There was a dense fog in the air; this was because the weather had cooled down a bit, and now an occasional breeze would come and go. But compared to the summer heat, it was very refreshing. Even the nights were cooler and perfect for taking a walk before it got dark. It was now really starting to feel like fall, even though it wasn't chilly like in other places. It still rained every now and then, but less frequently. Afterward, everything would change abruptly, from a rainy day to a sunny one, but still varied by each hour.

During breakfast, Trevor learned that they were going out for the second day in a row. But what he didn't know was that the place they were going to was somewhere no child should ever set foot in. There was a reason for this, as it had to do with one of Trevor's former adversaries, and this would help him finally leave his past behind.

"What's the plan for today, Uncle?" asked Margaret. "We have to go somewhere again, but I believe it will be very helpful for Trevor in forgetting about his previous life," Norman answered.

"Are you referring to the liquor store in Miami?" inquired Rhonda.

"No, this place is far worse, and while I don't think it's a good idea to bring Trevor along, I think it will be very beneficial for him," Norman replied.

"If you say so, Uncle, but I just hope it's not too much for Trevor to handle. He's already been through enough trauma," Margaret said.

"You don't have to worry about anything, because we'll be with him the entire time, and there are people there who will protect him if they have to," Norman reassured them.

"I don't like the sound of this place, whatever it might be. Maybe it would be better if we didn't go at all," Birdie told them.

"Who is this person that you're talking about, sir?" asked Trevor. "I don't want to tell you just yet, but trust me that once we leave, you'll feel much safer and at ease," Norman answered.

When they finished breakfast, they all got into the car and drove to the maximum-security prison near the fairgrounds. They went right inside where a security guard was waiting for them.

"You must be the one who I talked to over the phone. I must warn you, sir, this place may not be suitable for your child," the security guard told him.

"I am well aware of that, but the person we're here to see is someone that he knows. If you can take us to him now so that my young friend here can visit with him for a little while," Norman added.

"Very well, but I must also warn you that he's been screaming a lot lately, and we've tried everything to keep him quiet, but that doesn't seem to work. Alright, follow me," the security guard began.

He then led the way through a door that he unlocked with a key, and they went into an area with cells filled with people. Both the floor and walls were made of stone. As they passed by the different cells, Trevor looked very afraid. When they got to the last cell, which had Albert Swindle inside, he was clutching his burns, which were all bandaged up, and he was screaming.

The Unforgiven Hand

"I am just a simple businessman. You have to believe me! I don't want to hurt anyone!" Swindle yelled.

"Yes, that's me, I am here, Mr. Swindle," said Norman, looking around to see who called his name. "You have someone here that wants to see you," the security guard replied.

After seeing Albert Swindle sitting there, Trevor became even more afraid. "It's alright, Trevor, he won't hurt you, I promise," Norman told him.

"Do you want us to come inside with you?" asked Margaret.

"No, it's alright. I think I want Mr. Kingsley to because I would feel safer if he was with me," Trevor answered. It was then that the security guard unlocked the door to the cell, and both Trevor and Norman went in. "Trevor, my, how nice it is to see you again. Come closer so I can take a look at you and we can catch up on things," Albert Swindle said.

"I'm not afraid of him. Let me go alone," Trevor replied, and he started to walk toward Mr. Swindle. "You know, I never thought this would ever happen to me. When I was little, maybe close to your age, I became fascinated with magic, which became a longtime passion and why I started my business. But that's all ruined now. I'm never going to do another show ever again, and that makes me very sad because I really enjoyed performing in front of people. To tell you the truth, I hoped that it would take me further," Albert Swindle told him.

"What made you become so bad?" inquired Mr. Swindle inquired Trevor. "I don't really know. Perhaps it was something to do with my life growing up. I was very close to my mother but not so much to my father. He was a strict businessman who only cared about making money. We argued many times about what I wanted to be when I grew up. To make matters worse, my caravan burnt down, and now I have nothing left," Albert Swindle replied.

"I'm so sorry to hear that, sir. It was a very nice caravan, from what I can remember of it," Trevor added. "Can you ever forgive me for all the terrible things that I did to you?" inquired Mr. Swindle. "Oh yes, sir. I know that you didn't mean to do any of it, but when I think about it, I can't help but wonder why you did it," Trevor answered.

"That I can't tell you. Maybe at the time, I thought I was doing it because I was consumed by anger towards my father and that I didn't become as good of a magician as my rival Woodrow Wiggins, which, I believe, is why I murdered him," Albert Swindle began. "I always thought that you were a good magician, sir, and was honored to be your assistant even though it was only for a short time," Trevor said.

"Thank you, my boy, but there's no amount of kind words that can save me now. I have nothing left to live for. All of my pupils betrayed me, even Nathan. I always was very fond of him and should have treated him and the rest of you better. But the stress of being a businessman really got to me, and I never meant to take it out on you or any of my pupils," Mr. Swindle replied.

"Is that the truth, sir?" asked Trevor. "Yes, I'm afraid so. When I found out that my caravan had burnt down, I was devastated. I spent all of my life savings to buy it, and because I was so careless and turned to smoking cigars as a way to deal with my stress, I never thought it would be what would cause such a terrible thing to happen. I could have stopped at any time, but the cravings were uncontrollable. I don't expect a child like you to understand something like that," Albert Swindle answered.

"No, sir, I don't, but it does make a lot of sense to me. Although you never did that when I was around," Trevor added. "Do you remember that box that I had in my room in the caravan?" inquired Mr. Swindle. "Yes, sir, I do, really well. It's where you kept all of your money," Trevor replied. "Well, before the caravan burnt down, I hid the box somewhere so that the money would be safe. If you come closer, I will whisper to you where it is," Albert Swindle told him.

It was then that Trevor started walking toward Mr. Swindle, but before he could tell Trevor the whereabouts of the box, Norman raced and put out his arm to hold Trevor back. "For God's sake, man, you're about to die. The least that you can do is repent for all the bad that you've done," Norman began. At that point, Trevor picked up Mr. Swindle's hand, but Swindle started screaming in pain because of the burns on it, and the inmate in the next cell banged on the wall for him to stop.

"God, please forgive this horrible man and all the terrible things that he did," Trevor said. "Do you think he could possibly be forgiven?" asked Birdie. "No, it's inevitable. Even if that could happen, that doesn't justify any of his atrocious actions," Margaret answered. "Let me show you one last trick, Trevor, my boy, if you would let me do that as my last request," Albert Swindle told him.

"There will be no more of your tricks, Swindle. What you did to this boy is unforgivable. We're only here for him to see you one last time, but don't think if you show remorse now it will help make things better, because it won't," Norman began. "I can tell that he's being sincere about wanting me to forgive him. Even though he's a bad man, I still feel like I should forgive him," Trevor said.

"If that's what you want to do, then it's fine by us. But I think that you might want to think it over for a few minutes before making your final decision," Margaret replied. "Why do you think I should do that?" inquired Trevor. "Because if you think back to all the terrible things he's done not only to you but also to other children, as well, that's a good enough reason to," Rhonda replied.

"What's it going to be, Trevor, my boy?" asked Mr. Swindle. "I have to admit that I was very conflicted about what to do. But since it's my decision, I feel like it's only right to forgive Mr. Swindle. After all, I always believed that even if someone in your life does wrong to you, it's better just to forgive them than to be angry and hold a grudge against them," Trevor answered.

"Is that your final decision?" inquired Norman. "Yes, sir, it is. I know you may not agree with me, but I don't want to leave here without being able to say a proper goodbye to Mr. Swindle and to tell him that I'm not angry with him," Trevor replied. "That's a good boy. You made me very proud. I couldn't have asked for a more loyal pupil than you. If only we had stayed together, then the two of us would have accomplished so many great things," Albert Swindle told him.

"Perhaps so, but if that were to happen, Trevor's life would still be in danger. And had he not gotten away from you and found us, he might not have had anyone else in this world that he could trust," Norman began. "I must tell you, Trevor, my boy, that out of all of my pupils, you were my favorite of them all. And even though you ended up getting wounded because of me, I didn't intend to get you involved with my rivalry with Woodrow Wiggins. It's just that when he showed up that night, I needed you more than anything to be my backup because I knew that I couldn't rely on Nathan to do it," Mr. Swindle said.

"Do you really mean that, sir?" asked Trevor.

"Yes, I do, very much so. I had other pupils after you, but they didn't mean as much to me as you did. In fact, I wished you would come back to me so that you could continue your training and become as good of a magician as I am," Albert Swindle answered.

"Flattery won't do you any good, Swindle. You know this is the end of the road for you and that there's nothing you can say or do to make amends with all the bad things that you did. It's better if you just accept your fate," Norman told him.

"Why must my life be filled with nothing but suffering and misery?" inquired Mr. Swindle.

"I really do feel bad for you, sir, and was hoping that things would eventually turn around for you so that you could live a happy life," Trevor replied.

"That's very kind of you to say, my boy, but maybe in a way this is just how it had to happen. And I don't blame anyone for it. I just wish that I would have been as successful as my rival was. I don't know what it was about him, but he had something special that I didn't have," Albert Swindle added.

"What do you think it was?" asked Norman.

"I wish I knew because if I did, then I wouldn't have been so down on my luck and think that I've always been cursed since birth. And that there was never any way for me to be able to bounce back when it came to my career as a magician. Perhaps I should have just switched professions to something that suited me more, but I didn't want to give up what I was doing because I enjoyed doing it," Mr. Swindle answered.

"That was a good idea, sir. You should never give up something that you really enjoy even though it didn't make you a lot of money," Trevor began.

"Yes, I do know that, but I never thought it wouldn't work out in my favor. I'm a complete failure and am not ashamed to admit it," Albert Swindle said. "But there was something that I did succeed in, and that was gaining more pupils."

"Those two runaway children that you employed by manipulating them to join you. That was a very wrong thing to do. They should have chosen what path they wanted to take," Norman replied.

"How long have you known about that?" inquired Mr. Swindle.

"Not too long, but once we got Trevor back, he told us everything. I still don't understand why a grown man like you would want to prey on innocent children, of all the people in this world," Norman replied.

"Why did you choose children to do your bidding, sir?" asked Trevor.

"Maybe it's because I knew that no adults would do it, and it was much easier to target children because they're so vulnerable and will do anything that adults tell them to," Albert Swindle answered.

"That's still no excuse to do such a despicable thing. I, for one, will be happy when you're dead," Norman told him.

"To be honest with you, I'm a little bit scared about dying. I never used to be, but that was because back then I never used to worry about it that much. I always thought that I would die of old age," Mr. Swindle added.

It was then that the security guard went into the cell. "You have only a few minutes left, so you need to start wrapping things up soon," he began, then he exited and locked the door again. "Do you have anything else you want to say?" Trevor inquired.

"Not that I can think of, but looking back now and seeing all the wrong that I've done, I regret it all. I wish that I could somehow make up for it. Knowing that I can't makes me feel like such a heel," Albert Swindle replied.

"You should. All those children that you used for your own personal gain didn't deserve to be mistreated. But you took advantage of the fact that they didn't know any better, as a way to grow your business and make money. It was just deplorable," Norman said.

"It wasn't like I had a choice. The truth is, before I employed children, I was a very lonely man who never married or had children of my own. That was due to the fact that I was too focused on running my business to settle down and have a family. But I wish now that I wasn't so obsessed with that and could have made time for it," Mr. Swindle replied.

"Is that the real reason why you used children to work for you?" inquired Trevor.

"I'm afraid it is. There's no sense in lying about it now that I'm close to death. It's been weighing on my conscience ever since I've been in this prison. But I guess that doesn't matter anymore because my fate is sealed, and soon I will be no more, and the world will be a better place," Albert Swindle answered.

"Why don't you try asking God for forgiveness?" asked Norman.

"Even if I did, I'm still going to die regardless, so I feel that it's not worth doing. Not even God will show mercy on me for what I've done. It can't be undone or fixed. I should just be strong and brave, although it's very hard for me to do," Mr. Swindle replied.

"If it makes you feel any better, sir, I, too, fear death. When I was lying wounded in that field after you left me, I was certain that I was going to die. It scared me to think that someone as young as me could die. So I kind of know how you feel," Trevor told him.

"Do you really mean that, my boy?" inquired Albert Swindle.

"Oh yes, sir. Had I not found Mr. Kingsley and his two nieces, I might have died. I remember how hard it was to crawl while I was injured, but I never gave up hope because I knew that there had to be someone nice enough to help me," Trevor answered.

"Your time is up. Say goodbye," the security guard told them.

"Goodbye, Mr. Swindle. I hope that someday God can forgive you," Trevor said, and then they left. Albert Swindle went back to screaming again, and the prisoner in the next cell banged on the wall again to tell him to stop. Mr. Swindle knew that even though he felt guilty for his crimes and believed that by doing that he had redeemed himself, none of that mattered because Albert Swindle was going to be executed. He just didn't know when it would be.

The time drew nearer, and as it did, Mr. Swindle tried his best to be brave, even though he didn't know how much longer he had left to live. It was becoming nerve-racking for him, especially when he thought about it. But Albert Swindle was not the kind of person who wanted to be fearful. However, when the thought crossed his mind, Swindle felt that made it much harder for him, to the point where he felt sick to his stomach.

Mr. Swindle knew that it was only right that he paid the price for all the crimes that he had committed, but he couldn't help but wish that things could have turned out differently. If Albert Swindle had a conscience at all, then he might not have done what he did. And now, it was all catching up to him. The worst part about it was that he wouldn't live to see his next birthday, when he was going to turn fifty years old. In a way, he couldn't imagine himself to be that age because it seemed like only yesterday that he was a young boy with not a care in the world. He longed for those days and wished that there was some way to return to them again.

Even though his career as a magician was over, he didn't get the money that was promised to him, and he was on death row. Albert Swindle couldn't quite grasp the fact that his life was about to soon come to an end. There was a part of him that was full of regret; it was eating him up inside so much that it was driving him insane. This made him constantly pace the floor of his cell and mutter things to himself. The stage was set, and there was nothing left except for the execution chamber, the witness, and the eerie stench of death.

CHAPTER 19

Coming Full Circle

What had transpired in the previous chapter was now old news, and Trevor found himself in the midmorning feeling happiness that he had never felt before, which kept him in good spirits throughout the whole day. As the hours went by, everything was as it should be; however, that didn't last because Norman got a phone call from his friend Mr. Greenfield that the police had finally found and arrested Spyder. While this made him very happy to hear, there was more to it. The police were going to bring Spyder over to them, for what reason only Norman knew. The odd thing about all this was the place where Spyder had been caught: he was at a local store when someone had spotted him and called the police. At first, Spyder denied his identity, that is, until they went through his wallet and found something that confirmed who he really was. And now that Spyder had been caught, the last piece of the puzzle was going to be put in place.

In the early afternoon, Trevor helped Margaret plant some new flowers around the backyard. A little bit after they got washed up, they had lunch. "Trevor, I'm afraid I have some rather sad news. They executed Albert Swindle this morning," Margaret said. "They said that he was very cooperative and his last words before they gave him the lethal injection were 'I don't want to be remembered for all my misdeeds but for who I was as a person,'" Norman began.

"This is such depressing news to hear, and I know that he was a bad man, but I have a feeling that God finally forgave him," Trevor said. "I believe so, too, because he seemed very remorseful when we saw him yesterday, but maybe it had something to do with the fact that he was going to die and wanted to repent," Margaret replied.

Just then, there was a knock at the door. "Who do you think it is?" asked Rhonda. "I think that I know. Let me answer it. You two take Trevor into the living room, and I will meet you in there shortly," Norman answered. They all got up from the table. Norman went to answer the door while Margaret and Birdie went with Trevor into the living room. Within a few minutes, he went into the living room, along with a policeman and Mr. Greenfield, all with a serious look on their faces.

"What's going on, Uncle?" inquired Margaret. "All will be explained very soon, but all that I can tell you is this will be the final stage in all that we've been dealing with. Alright, you can bring him in now," Norman replied.

Just then, another policeman went into the room with Spyder. "That's the man from the post office that I was telling you about," Trevor told them, standing up. "It's alright, my dear child, he can't hurt you in any way," Norman added. "Oh, it's you. I've had just about enough of you already. If it wasn't for you meddling, my plan would have worked," Spyder began.

"We know who you are, Percy Becker. There's no need to keep pretending. We also knew about your plan to kill Trevor to obtain the money in the will, which rightfully belongs to him," Margaret said. "There's no way you could have known that was only for me to know," Spyder replied. "That is a lie. Besides working alongside Ferguson, you were also in cahoots with Mr. Albert Swindle, as well," Mr. Greenfield told him.

"I don't know anyone with that name. You must have me confused with someone else," Spyder added.

"Then perhaps this should clear things up. Your father, Ronald, and his wife, Agatha, had you a few years before another baby girl was born. She later married a man named Malcolm Donner, and they had a child together. But unfortunately, the woman died unexpectedly," Norman began.

"What are you implying?" asked Spyder.

"Nothing, but on the day of the child's birth, his mother was wearing a gold wedding ring on her finger that was stolen by one of the church employees. It was then given to another employee and somehow found its way to you," Mr. Greenfield said.

"I don't know anything about a wedding ring or any church, for that matter, and that's the truth," Spyder replied.

"Do you know a Pastor Swanson?" inquired Norman.

"Not that I can say. I haven't been to church for many years and have no intention of ever going again," Spyder replied.

"Well, he knows you, and apparently, you were also working with him and his wife. The three of you met down in Miami, and during that time, the ring was given to you," Margaret told him.

"I was never in Miami, nor would I do business with a pastor, of all people. It's absurd to even think of such a thing," Spyder added.

"It's clear to us that you're doing things under false pretenses, but we have proof because both Pastor Swanson and his wife signed a confession admitting to what they did. They, like you, tried to act as though they were innocent. It wasn't easy, but after a while, we were able to get the truth out of them," Mr. Greenfield began.

"What do you want me to do?" asked Spyder.

"You must also sign a confession as evidence that you were involved," Norman answered.

"I will do no such thing, and there isn't anyone that can make me," Spyder said.

"Do you know the name of the woman we're talking about?" inquired Margaret.

"No, I don't, nor do I really care," Spyder replied.

"You just might if we were to tell you. That might just help," Rhonda told him.

"Her name was Grace, and she was my younger sister and your second cousin, which makes Trevor here your first cousin," Norman added.

"That can't be true. This boy isn't related to me in any way. I know my family's history very well," Spyder began.

"Obviously not, because I did some research, which is how I found out. You can deny it all you want, but Norman has the papers in his office to prove it," Mr. Greenfield said.

"I don't believe that unless you show them to me," Spyder replied.

"There's no need for that. You know what we're saying is the truth," Birdie told him.

"Do you still have the ring in your possession?" asked Norman.

"No, and even if I did, I wouldn't give it to you," Spyder answered.

"We need to know what you did with it. Tell us right now," Mr. Greenfield told him.

"Fine. If you must know, I threw it into Biscayne Bay because I thought at the time that by doing it, that boy's identity would never be revealed," Spyder added.

"But you didn't count on the fact that our uncle was one step ahead of you and was able to find out that information on his own, so we never needed the ring in the first place," Margaret began.

"Damn you all to hell! I put in a lot of time and effort to come up with my plan. Had it not been for that boy or any of you interfering, it might not have failed," Spyder said.

"You can't put the blame on anyone else but yourself. There was no way for you to obtain the money from the will because it is somewhere that you would never find. Only I myself know," Norman replied.

"This is all Swindle's fault. If he had not persuaded me to be partners with him, I might have gotten what I wanted. I never needed him or that group of vagabonds to help me. I would have just been better working alone," Spyder told them.

"You can't put the blame entirely on Swindle because you and all those who worked alongside you are all guilty," Mr. Greenfield added. "That's right. This whole thing was your idea from the start. You reap what you sow, which means that this is all on you," Margaret began.

"How can I have been so incautious with my plan?" inquired Spyder.

"It's not that you were too overconfident. It was that you never once considered that there were a lot of flaws," Norman replied.

"You don't have to tell me that this whole thing backfiring wasn't what I expected. And had I gone about my plan a different way, it wouldn't have been thwarted by that little twerp or any of you. After all, your sister owes me a lot," Spyder began.

"She owes you nothing. You, sir, are a psychotic maniac who needs help. That much is certain," Mr. Greenfield said.

"Are you going to agree to sign the confession?" asked Norman.

"Alright, if it gets me out of here quicker," Spyder answered.

It was then that Norman placed the confession paper onto the table and handed Spyder a pen, with which he signed the paper. "I hope you learned a lesson from all of this. Crime never pays. I have spoken to the chief of police, and he has informed me that you will be relocated to California. There is a prison there that already agreed to take you," Norman told him.

"Fine then. The further away from you fools, the better. I've been wanting to get out of this state for a while now, and it looks like I'm finally going to get my wish," Spyder told them.

"Do you have anything else that you would like to say?" asked Mr. Greenfield.

"The only thing that comes to mind is that I curse the day that boy was born. And know that this isn't over. Not by a long shot. I'm going to keep making all of your lives a living hell. So much, in fact, that it will drive you to the brink of insanity," Spyder replied.

"Alright, you can take him away now," Norman ordered. At that point, Spyder was escorted out by the policemen.

"It's official now. Neither Spyder nor Albert Swindle can ever hurt Trevor again. I'm just happy that we don't have to worry about them anymore," Margaret added.

"Yes, but what I don't understand is what Spyder meant when he said that my sister owed me," Norman began.

"He probably was just saying that to make us believe that there was something more involved in this. But I'm certain that it was a lie," Rhonda said.

"Where is the will that my parents left?" inquired Trevor.

"I suppose it would only be right to show you now. If you would follow me," Norman answered. They all got up and followed Norman into his office. When they got there, Norman pulled three books off the shelf, revealing a medium-size box. "Is that where you kept the will?" asked Birdie.

"Yes, once I figured out who was missing from the family tree, which, if you remember, I researched to find out about Trevor's family history, I hid it there just in case someone like Percy tried to cheat our young friend here out of the money that rightfully belongs to him," Norman replied.

"Why didn't you tell us about this before, Uncle?" inquired Margaret.

"I thought about doing that but wanted to wait until it was all over before I could reveal the location to you all," Norman answered. He then pulled out a piece of paper from the box and handed it to Mr. Greenfield. "What does it say?" asked Rhonda.

"There's a lot on here, but the most important thing is that Trevor's parents left him three thousand dollars to be deposited into a savings account that will be made for our son so that he is always financially secure for the rest of his life," Mr. Greenfield replied.

"What does that mean, sir?" inquired Trevor.

"That you will never have to worry about money problems ever again," Norman explained. "I will continue to hold on to this, and when I have free time, I will go to the bank and open up the savings account for Trevor," Mr. Greenfield added as he handed the will back to Norman, who put it back in the box and returned it to its hiding place behind the three books.

"Now that we know that the will is safe and there's no more left to try and steal it, I guess it's safe to say that we're finally in the clear," Norman told them. "Yes, I should be going home now because I have a few things to do, but I will call you in a couple of days, Norman, and we'll discuss making plans. Goodbye, everyone," Mr. Greenfield added, and then he left.

"What should we do now?" inquired Margaret.

"I have an idea. Since it's already October and Halloween is tomorrow, the two of us have been talking and think that it would be fun if we took Trevor trick-or-treating for the first time in his life. So we're going to take him out to a store so that he can pick out his own costume," Rhonda suggested.

"I like the idea a lot, and I think that it will be fun for Trevor. And since you two are willing to take him, I can pass out candy to the trick-or-treaters who come by," Norman added.

"We better be on our way then, so that we have enough time to make dinner when we come home. We will only be out for an hour," Margaret said. "What store are we going to?" asked Trevor.

"There's one that we know of that's not too far from here and has good prices, but they close at seven, so there's only a few hours left," Birdie replied.

It was at that point that they left. Trevor looked at a few different costumes, but there was a clown one that caught his eye. They also bought makeup, some decorations, and a pumpkin. When they got home, Margaret and Rhonda made dinner. They planned to get up early so that they could spend the morning decorating and carve the pumpkin, which they were going to display on the front porch.

Trevor was so excited about going trick-or-treating for the first time that he agreed to also get up early to help Margaret and Birdie decorate. With no more threats to be concerned about, they could finally live their lives together, knowing that Trevor was free from harm. This gave them a great sense of relief.

With a great weight lifted off their shoulders, Trevor knew that he had no reason to fear. Because of that, he could live the rest of his life in harmony, which was the best part of it all. In the next few days, Norman was going to deposit the money that Trevor's parents left him in their will. If we were to look back on the journey that Trevor had been on, it would make you believe in miracles.

He started out as a penniless orphan who was forced into a life of poverty without the confines of the strict church he was born in. But after going through so many other hardships, Trevor had miraculously persevered through it all. By doing so, he had gained the unconditional love of a family that gave him the sense of belonging he had been searching for. He had shown the true meaning of the indomitable human spirit and how to use it to overcome adversity.

Had it not been for that, Trevor would have had to continue down the road of unhappiness. But now that was all water under the bridge, and the future looked bright for Trevor because he and his life were finally coming full circle.

CHAPTER 20

At Last

For those fortunate enough to survive the horrific acts detailed in this story, which concluded, those affected had found peace of mind. However, the remnants of the former group of villains, now reduced in number, underwent a significant transformation from their humble beginnings. The months leading up to Albert Swindle's demise could be summarized succinctly.

Now that circumstances had improved, and within that timeframe, before Norman met Trevor, Norman held a low opinion of children. This was because of his rigid nature, emphasizing subjects like politics, making him intolerant of anyone else's opinions but his own. However, Trevor somehow managed to change his heart. The specific trigger wasn't crucial because by adopting Trevor, Norman became more open-minded, especially toward children.

As indicated in the previous chapter, Trevor was thrilled about going trick-or-treating, so much so that he jumped out of bed when he woke up. Unsure whether to put on his costume immediately, he kept his pajamas on. Trevor proceeded downstairs and outside, where Margaret and Rhonda were busy decorating the exterior of the house.

"Can I help?" asked Trevor.

"Sure you can. We'll do the ones that have to be hung high up. Here you go, you can do these," Margaret replied.

"Where should we put these?" inquired Birdie.

"I was thinking, by the upstairs windows, and we can put the rest in the yard. The door we can do last," Margaret replied.

They worked until there were no more decorations to put up, then they went inside to have breakfast.

"Do you think it's going to rain today?" asked Margaret.

"I hope not because then we can't take Trevor trick-or-treating. But the weather report said that it's only supposed to be cloudy," Rhonda answered.

"I was thinking that we could make cookies and decorate them for Halloween," Margaret began. "Would it be alright if I helped you?" Trevor inquired.

"Of course, you can. We'll start sometime in the afternoon so that they'll be done before dinner, and we can have them for dessert. We'll have to go to the store after breakfast to get what we need," Birdie replied. "If you want, you can come with us, Trevor. That way, you can help us pick out what kind of decorations we can use," Margaret said.

"Yes, I would really like to. I just have to go upstairs to change, and I will be right back down in a few minutes," Trevor replied, then went back upstairs to change out of his pajamas.

It was a little bit after they ate breakfast that they all went down the street to the store. Trevor saw a few people dressed up.

Trevor and the ladies had cookie dough and orange-and-black frosting with matching sprinkles. After they got home, there was only one more hour left until the afternoon came. Trevor saw some other children who were playing soccer in the front yard at the house across the street from them, so he joined them. They taught him how to play, and by the time the game was over, Trevor was very tired. He rested for a little while.

When it was the afternoon and time to start making the cookies, Trevor assisted. "What can I do?" asked Trevor.

"You can help me with the cookie dough. I'll cut it, and you can put it onto the baking sheet," Rhonda answered.

Suddenly they saw Norman going downstairs, he seemed to be joyful. "What do I smell?" he inquired.

"We're baking Halloween cookies to have after dinner," Margaret replied. "You three can have them. I don't feel like eating anything with sugar," Norman told them.

"When are we going to go out trick-or-treating?" asked Trevor.

"Later on, after dinner," Birdie answered. "I got a call this morning from the police department. They wanted to update me on things," Norman said.

"Do you mean about our cousin?" inquired Margaret.

"Yes, they have informed me that he is on a special plane for convicts out to California and should arrive in another five hours from now," Norman replied.

"Oh, sir, I couldn't be happier to hear something like that because he made me very afraid," Trevor added.

"You don't have to call me sir anymore. We're a family now," Norman began. "What should I call you then?" asked Trevor.

"How about Mr. Kingsley? That seems appropriate and is easy for you to remember," Norman answered.

"What else did the police say?" inquired Rhonda.

"They told me that Percy is going to be doing ten years and, after that, will be eligible for parole, depending on how he behaves while in prison," Norman replied.

"I couldn't help but notice that you brought the old portrait of your sister from out of the attic. We need to wipe all of the dust off it before we can hang it up," Margaret said.

"Where do you plan to hang the portrait, uncle?" asked Birdie.

"I was considering the living room above the couch because I don't have any more room on the walls in my office," Norman answered. "That would be a fantastic place. There's already a picture hanging, but it's not a very good painting, so we can take that down and replace it with the portrait of Aunt Grace," Margaret told them.

"Why did you take it down from the attic, Mr. Kingsley?" inquired Trevor.

"I thought it would be nice to honor her memory, and that way, every time you look at the portrait, it will help you feel less sad," Norman replied.

"How do you figure that, Uncle?" asked Margaret.

"Well, even though Trevor didn't know his mother, he should know that she's watching over him," Norman answered.

"When are you going to put the picture on the wall?" asked Trevor.

"Later, while you are out trick-or-treating, so when you come home, you can go into the living room to look at it," Norman replied. "I noticed that in the portrait, Aunt Grace was wearing the same wedding ring that is now at the bottom of Biscayne Bay," Rhonda added. "I actually did notice that, but at first, I thought it was a different ring until I looked more closely," Margaret began.

Once the cookies started baking in the oven, Trevor worked on a Halloween-themed maze for the children. They ate a late lunch, and afterward, Trevor started another maze because he had already finished the first one. By the time early evening arrived, he had a few others completed. Trevor tried to contain his excitement but found it very difficult. He continued to work on the mazes until night fell. That was when some children who were trick-or-treating went to their door. Margaret and Birdie were busy making dinner but took turns answering the door and giving out candy.

"Is dinner ready yet?" Trevor inquired as he entered the kitchen. "No, it will be in a few minutes. You should wash up," Margaret answered. Just then, the doorbell rang again. "Do you want me to get that?" asked Rhonda. "Yes, and when you come back, can you go to Uncle Norman's office and tell him that dinner will be ready soon?" Margaret replied. Birdie left to answer the door while Trevor washed up and then sat down at the kitchen table. Norman and Birdie entered the kitchen together. "What's for dinner tonight, ladies?" asked Norman. "Something that we haven't had for a while—spaghetti with meatballs with garlic bread," Margaret answered. Norman got a drink from the refrigerator and then sat down at the table. "Are the cookies done yet?" inquired Trevor. "Yes, they should be ready in time for dessert," Rhonda replied.

After dinner, Trevor went right upstairs to his room and put on his clown costume. When he returned downstairs, Margaret painted Trevor's face, and Trevor went back into the kitchen. "How do I look?" he asked. "Great, as if you're all ready to go trick-or-treating. We're almost done cleaning up, then we'll go," Margaret answered. "I'm going to Mr. Kingsley's office right now to show him, too," Trevor began. He then left to go into Norman's office to show him his costume.

As they were leaving to go trick-or-treating, they saw something fly by into the sky very fast. "Look, Trevor, it's a shooting star. You can make a wish on it, and if you're lucky enough, it might just come true," Birdie said. "I don't need to do that, because everything that I've ever wished for has already come true," Trevor replied.

"That makes us so happy to hear. We better be on our way now. Remember to stay close to Rhonda and myself at all times," Margaret told him, and they went out into the neighborhood. Trevor joined another group of children, and when they got home, Trevor was allowed to eat only one piece of candy. He then went into the living room, where Norman had just finished putting up the picture of

Trevor's mother on the wall. "What do you think?" he inquired. "It looks so good there, Mr. Kingsley, and I can see it better now than when we first found it in the attic," Trevor replied. "Yes, I happen to agree. Somehow, I had forgotten that it was in the attic. But since meeting you, this portrait will remain on this wall. The one that was hanging up before, I put in the corner of my bedroom closet until I can figure out what to do with it," Norman added.

It was then that Margaret and Birdie went into the room. "I see that you put up the picture of Aunt Grace. You know, I vaguely remember the last time that we saw her," Margaret began. "It was a few years ago; we went to her Christmas party, and she had cooked and baked everything herself," Rhonda said.

"Did you go trick-or-treating?" asked Norman. "Yes, I did, very much so, and even made a few friends who live in this neighborhood. I went with them for most of the time," Trevor answered. "One of their parents was nice enough to invite us all over for dinner next week on Thursday, and I already accepted their invitation," Margaret told them.

"How did you get all of the dust off the portrait, Uncle?" inquired Birdie. "I used an old handkerchief that I've had for a long time. There was so much of it that it took me an hour to finish, and then I went into the garage, got a hammer and some nails, and replaced the old picture with this one," Norman replied.

"Should I bring in the pumpkin from the porch?" asked Margaret. "No, let's leave it out for a little while longer, and one of us can bring it in at the end of the night," Rhonda answered. Just then, the doorbell rang again. "That must be some more trick-or-treaters. Allow me to go and give out the candy so that you two can have a little break," Norman added.

"Can I be the one who does it?" asked Trevor. "Alright, I have to grab the bowl of candy that's by the door," Norman replied. Trevor then went with Norman to answer the door and pass out candy to the trick-or-treaters. Then he went back into the living room, where Margaret and Birdie were now sitting down on the couch.

"Do you think there will be more trick-or-treaters?" inquired Rhonda. "I hope not because I'm exhausted and think that I will go upstairs to sleep very soon," Margaret replied. "I feel that way and also will be heading up to bed in a little while," Birdie told them.

"Shouldn't we bring the pumpkin and take down the decorations?" asked Trevor. "We can leave them until tomorrow morning. Well, I am ready to go get some sleep. Good night," Margaret answered, and then she got up and went upstairs to her room. "That sounds like a really good idea, and I think I'll do the same. Good night, Trevor dear," Rhonda added, and she got up and went upstairs. He was left alone because Norman had gone back into his office again.

Trevor decided to go upstairs to his room. On the way there, he ran into Norman, who had the bowl of candy in his hand. "Where did Margaret and Birdie go?" he inquired. "They went to sleep because they were both tired," Trevor replied. "I can see why. You all woke up early, and I thought that you would be tired, too, and had gone to sleep already," Norman began.

"No, I am wide-awake and was just going to go to my room since I finished all of my Halloween mazes earlier. I'm trying to decide what I should do until I get tired and am ready to fall asleep," Trevor said. "If you want, I have an old laptop that I don't use anymore. You can play some free games for children on the internet. I can help you find them," Norman replied.

"Are you going to sleep soon too?" asked Trevor. "No, I still have important things to take care of first, but I will get you the laptop. It's upstairs on my dresser in my room," Norman answered. They went up together, and Norman lent his old laptop to Trevor and helped him find a few different sites to play games that were for children. Trevor played until he started to feel tired and fell asleep in his clown costume.

In the end, things had worked out for the best. Trevor had gotten everything he had once dreamed of. While he used to be looked at as a charity case and was all alone in this world, Trevor had overcome so many obstacles to get what he desired the most, which was to find people who would be kind and take care of him.

You must be wondering what happened to some of the other characters. It was because Nathan informed Trevor of Albert Swindle's plan and testified against him that Nathan received a pardon and was eventually adopted by a loving family that already had children of its own. Now, Nathan was happy and got along well with his adopted parents and siblings and even got enrolled in school, where he took classes every day.

As for Ezra Cooper, also known as Robert Porter, he drifted from place to place and never really amounted to anything after they escaped from the police. He and Zoey lost touch with each other. However, she found someone else, and they started dating, which later led to their engagement and then marriage. Zoey had two children, a boy and a girl who were twins. She spent her days staying at home; she took up painting and sold her paintings to make money.

Pastor Swanson and his wife lost their jobs at the church after the government found out about their deplorable behavior toward the children and their affiliation with Spyder. They were forced to live in a mobile home and became poor and miserable, just like what happened before to the children whom they mistreated and abused for such a long time.

Doc had unexpectedly betrayed Brock Ferguson, and as a result of his heroic act, he was given the Carnegie Medal. The police helped him find some family members of his who were living, and they were generous enough to let him live with them.

Joseph Bishop Briggs disappeared and was never seen or heard from ever again. He was presumed to be dead; however, someone had claimed to have seen him at a local public house, but it wasn't certain.

Last but not least, Zeke, the bartender, moved back to his hometown of Atlanta, Georgia, where he became a policeman but was shot dead while confronting a group of gang members who were attempting to mug a woman on the street.

Although Trevor was safe from any malicious people, he won't ever forget the scowl on Spyder's face, the brooding Brock Ferguson, or the stuffed heads that were all over the walls of Mr. Swindle's caravan. But with all that had occurred, it had become a distant memory. And through all the hardships, there was a silver lining that, like a rainbow after a rainstorm, Trevor had finally fulfilled his destiny, and for once in Trevor's life, all was well.

www.ingramcontent.com/pod-product-compliance
Lightning Source LLC
LaVergne TN
LVHW091544060526
838200LV00036B/697